The Hopscotch Tree

OTHER YEARLING BOOKS YOU WILL ENJOY:

YEARLING BOOKS are designed especially to entertain and enlighten young people. Patricia Reilly Giff, consultant to this series, received her bachelor's degree from Marymount College and a master's degree in history from St. John's University. She holds a Professional Diploma in Reading and a Doctorate of Humane Letters from Hofstra University. She was a teacher and reading consultant for many years, and is the author of numerous books for young readers.

For a complete listing of all Yearling titles, write to
Dell Readers Service,
P.O. Box 1045,
South Holland, IL 60473.

The Hopscotch Tree

LEDA SISKIND

A Yearling Book

The publisher wishes to thank the YIVO
Library for help with the Yiddish that appears
in this book.

Published by
Bantam Doubleday Dell Books for Young Readers
a division of
Bantam Doubleday Dell Publishing Group, Inc.
1540 Broadway
New York, New York 10036

ISBN: 0-440-40959-4

Reprinted by arrangement with Bantam Books for Young Readers

Printed in the United States of America

October 1995

10 9 8 7 6 5 4 3 2 1

OPM

*For my parents within these pages and
for Larry and Elizabeth*

Chapter One

I could see the Purple Sweater coming toward me from across the schoolyard and my stomach did that melted cheese thing again. I mean my stomach just oozed hot and drippy inside and then melted away. Then I stood there in the middle of the playground feeling as if I had no stomach at all. I wanted to run to the Hopscotch Tree, but I couldn't move.

"Ha-ee-ee-y, *Edith*!"

I squinted to see Zandra's face, but she was still too far away, and besides, I really didn't need to see what she looked like. I could tell she was grinning. I could hear the grin in her voice. Behind the Purple Sweater was her gang of four girls running to catch up with her. They were laughing and zipping up their jackets. One of them, the one I called the

Boxer, was punching circles into the air with her fists. The setting sun made the fists' shadows long and twirling on the asphalt.

"Hey, *E-E-E-dith!*" Zandra yelled again. The Purple Sweater had this way of traveling across a playground as if she were pushing off to roller skate every time she took a step. I really wished I could just turn around and run away, but I couldn't move. It was always like this. It had been like this for weeks now, ever since I had come to Layton Street School.

Daddy had said there was no better way to begin 1960 than by starting out fresh in our new house, even if the year *was* almost over. So we had left our tiny apartment and come over to this side of town. But this side of town had this stupid school—and the Purple Sweater to go with it.

They surrounded me. The Boxer and the Tall Girl began pushing me backward. Not hard, but I knew where we were heading. They wanted me up against the back fence, at the rear of the school, by the side steps of the upper-grade building. The other two girls—I think they were sisters—kept laughing as Zandra plucked little fuzzy balls off her bulky purple sweater and threw them in my face. I felt the diamond-shaped steel holes of the fence against my back. We stopped.

Zandra's green eyes tore across my face as if she were looking for something she couldn't find. She just about purred every time she spoke to me. She reminded me of a mountain lion.

"Edith, we've been looking *all over* for you, haven't we?"

"Uh-huh," said the Boxer. She kept slamming one of her fists into her palm.

"We went by the Softball Tree, the Tether Ball Trees, we even went by the handball court. But you never play handball, do you, Edith," Zandra said. "No, you hide out by the Hopscotch Tree, all the way back here, don't you, Edith. You think you're too good for us!"

I couldn't say anything. I could've screamed a million things, I guess, but my mouth was stuck shut. By this time, my knees were shaking like the Coyote's do on the Road Runner cartoons just before a rock or something falls on him. Some marvelous picture *that* would make: Road Runner knees under a melted cheese stomach.

One of the sisters yanked down my braid and jerked my head back. I closed my eyes, but I was crying anyway.

"Do you think you're too good for us? Huh? You skinny little Jew, you *do,* don't you," Zandra hissed.

I felt the bony fingers of the Tall Girl hold my arm on one side and someone else grab my other arm.

"Open your eyes, you stupid kike!" Zandra shouted. I opened my eyes. Zandra stepped on my feet. She was like a monster crushing against me. "And remember, Edith Gold," Zandra began to sing in her low voice:

"You'd better not shout,
Don'tcha dare hide,
You'd better watch out,
I'm telling you why,
Zandra Kott is gonna get you-ooo.

"You understand, Jew girl? You tell anybody— *anybody*—you're too stuck up to bother with us and you'll wish you hadn't. You'll be dead meat."

"Dead meat," the Boxer repeated.

"Got that, Gold-steen, Gold-burg, Gold-styne, Gold-booger?" Zandra asked.

I nodded.

Zandra jumped off my feet. Then she snapped her fingers, galloped away with her gang, and disappeared.

My feet really hurt but I could still wriggle my toes. I wiped my eyes and turned to look at the Hopscotch Tree.

It had been watching me the whole time.

Even though it was a little windy, the Hopscotch Tree was absolutely still. Not one leaf was moving. The branches of all the other trees that lined the side of the playground were swaying slowly in the breeze, as they're supposed to do, I guess, because

they're just trees. But the Hopscotch Tree was different. It knew what had just happened and it was
waiting for me. I walked over.

The Hopscotch Tree was gigantic. It was the
largest living thing at Layton Street School. Its thick,
rough branches reached up way beyond the top of
the school's roofs and some of the Tree hung over
the fence and spread out above the sidewalk and the
street. Its trunk looked like a Y from far away. Up
close you could see that the trunk twisted around
itself in a swirl and then separated so that the two
main branches leaned out in opposite directions.
Right in the middle of the trunk was a smooth black
knot with a hole in it. I stood in front of the Tree
and put my hand on the knot. I closed my eyes and
pictured the Purple Sweater glaring down at me
again.

You saw that, didn't you? I asked silently. I looked
up. The sunset was sprinkled on the thousands and
thousands of little branches and leaves. The leaves
nodded. *She called me a kike,* I said. That's an
awful name for a Jew. My parents had told me
that saying "kike" was like calling someone a "nig-
ger" or something. *Did you hear her call me that?*
The Tree nodded once more. I closed my eyes
again. I saw my old school. I could see its white
Spanish-looking building and some of my old
friends—Lisa Rosen and Judy Nestlebaum and
Amy Cohen and—did we *have* to move? I leaned

5

my head back. The Tree was still and then nodded again. I rubbed the knot with my palm. *Okay, okay, okay, but if I have to be at this dumb school and I'm gonna get beat up, couldn't Zandra at least have picked another song? It's not even Thanksgiving yet and she's already singing that stupid Christmas song.* I heard a rustle and lifted my head. The Tree's branches were swinging back and forth. *No,* it said. So I guess Zandra couldn't have picked another song. *But what will I do?* I asked. *I can't tell anybody but you.* The Tree was still. It didn't have an answer. From where I stood, I could see hundreds of the Tree's seed pods dangling from the branches like brown crescent moons. When they fell to the ground, kids would pick them up and shake them to hear the rattle of the beans inside, or use them to mark their place on the hopscotch squares. But I knew that the pods held seeds for more trees inside them—and I knew that the Hop-scotch Tree would let me take one of its pods away for good luck. I found a long C-shaped pod at my feet.

"Thanks," I said aloud and put the pod inside my jacket pocket.

"Yoo-hoo! Edith!"

That voice was my mom's. Except when she was mad, my mom always sounded as if she were just about to break into a deep belly laugh. I ran back to the rear gate and out to the car. Mom opened the door for me and I slid in.

"Hello there, sweetie, how'd it go today? Edith? Edith? What are you staring at?"

"*You*," I said. "I like the way you look today. Your hair's up in a bun and you're wearing my favorite outfit with the little pearls."

Mom drove away from the curb. She laughed. "This old gray suit? I wouldn't have worn it except that we had a big meeting at the office this afternoon. It makes me look so drab."

"No, it doesn't!" I said. "You look like a principal or . . . or . . . somebody on TV. Really!" I was trying to tell my mom not to dress so kooky. She usually put on a lot of bright, bright colors and weird jewelry. She even wore her hair down in a couple of braids sometimes, like a girl.

"So how's school coming along?" Mom asked at a stoplight.

I looked down. "It's okay. I just still miss Silverlake, that's all." I guess I didn't *sound* okay because Mom gave me one of her soft-eyed looks and squeezed my hand.

"I know, hon, I know. It takes a while to get used to a new school and a whole new fifth-grade class." I could tell she was thinking of something happier to say.

"So, did you guys ever take that math quiz?"

7

I smiled. "Nope. She forgot. That's the best part about being in Mrs. Vanderbuildt's class—she forgets a lot."

Mom shook her head as we pulled into our driveway. *"Oy vey,"* she said, "and I suppose none of you are going to remind her of it, right?"

I grinned. "That's right."

I hopped out of the car and helped Mom unload some groceries from the trunk. Our new little house had these neat white columns and side porches with long windows. I did have to admit that living in a house with a backyard and porches and stuff sure did beat our tiny apartment in Silverlake. I loved our new kitchen most of all. It had yellow walls, floor, drawers, table and chairs. The only things not yellow were the white stove and refrigerator. It was like being inside of a cozy egg.

I lifted my bag onto the kitchen table and looked inside.

"Aw, Mom," I said. "Are we having lamb chops and peas *again?*"

Mom laughed and opened the refrigerator to put something in. "Yes we are, sweetie, sorry."

"We *always* have lamb chops and peas."

"We don't *always* have lamb chops and peas," Mom said. "Just on Fridays. *Somebody's* got to plan menus around here. And speaking of Friday, go get the Sabbath candles, will you?"

I took out the candles and the small golden candlesticks from the bottom drawer in the hall and brought them back into the kitchen. Mom set them up on the side counter.

"Now," Mom continued, "just as soon as Daddy—"

The front door slammed. "Hel-loh!" my father sang out. "Hel-loh!"

I ran into the living room. "Hey, Daddy!"

Daddy took off his painter's cap and kneeled down to hug me. "Hey! How are you, *Doosh-sheesh-ka*?" *Doosh-sheesh-ka* is Russian for "my little soul." Daddy was born in Russia and he always called me that. I could still smell the paint on his overalls when we hugged.

"I'm okay," I said, backing away. "You were using green today, right?"

He smiled. "That's right. Why? Do I look good in green?"

"Sure," I said as we walked into the kitchen. "That is, if you like it in your hair, on your nose, and on your eyelids."

"Hi, hon," Mom said.

"Hi, ya," Daddy said, and he gave Mom a little kiss on her cheek.

"We just took out the candles for Shabbat," Mom went on, "and if you wash up right now, we can light candles and eat in about twenty minutes."

"Sounds good to me," Daddy said. Then he went off to take a shower.

After Daddy was all clean and changed out of his

painter clothes, the three of us stood in front of the candlesticks and Mom struck a match. When the candles were lit, Mom circled her arms three times over them and then placed her hands over her eyes.

"Barukh Atah Adonai—" she began.

We didn't belong to a temple or anything and Daddy often said he wasn't real fond of religion, but we did light Sabbath candles. Mom had explained to me that lighting the candles at sunset and saying a prayer was a way of celebrating one week and looking forward to the next. And when the candles were glowing in the dark, it *was* like a tiny, tiny holiday every Friday. At the end of the prayer, we all kissed one another.

Well, I was thinking, at least dinner will be all right, even if after school wasn't. I was wrong. We were heading toward Uh-Oh Time.

Chapter Two

WE weren't very far into dinner when Mom said, "Edith, piling your peas into little circles and squares doesn't fool me, you know. Just eat your peas, please."

"They're in triangles," I said, because they were.

"Whatever," Mom said. "Just eat them. And sit up straight, please."

"When I was a boy in the Ukraine," Daddy said, "we didn't even *have* peas."

"You were lucky," I said, laughing.

Mom smiled. *"A knaker,"* she said. *Knaker* means "wiseguy" in Yiddish.

Daddy wiped his mouth with a napkin. "I might have some good news. If I can round up some of the fellas, I might get that new apartment complex across the street from the house I'm painting now. The owner came over and said he liked my work and was I free and all that."

Mom put down her glass. "That's great. We could sure use the money. Did you tell him you'd be the foreman? You could make more that way."

"Well . . ." Daddy said. You could tell he hadn't said that.

Mom frowned.

"Are we having Jell-O for dessert?" I asked. I was trying to stop the Uh-Oh because I could tell it was coming.

"Did you at least quote a higher rate?" Mom's voice became hard and flat.

Daddy sighed. "No. No, I didn't."

"If we're having Jell-O, I don't want it," I said.

"Why not?" Mom asked. She was staring straight at Daddy.

"Because it shakes too much," I said.

"Because I want the job," Daddy said. He let his fork clatter on the plate.

Mom stood up. "You're losing money, you know that? 'A roys gevorfn gelt'—money thrown out!"

" 'A noenter groshn iz beser vi a vayter kerbl!' " Daddy said loudly. " 'A penny in the hand is better than a dollar—' "

"Oh, really?" Mom was shouting. "Yiddish sayings? Is that what we're doing? Well, 'Gelt geyt tsu gelt.' 'Money goes *to* money,' okay? I don't know why you always—"

"I can't just—" Daddy started.

Uh-Oh Time was here. I hated it when my parents fought because I never knew what to do or who to be mad at. The fights were always about money and Daddy not working enough. I always felt as if it were my fault, too, somehow. And if I could just find the right thing to say or do, all the Uh-Oh in the air would go away.

Suddenly Daddy pushed his chair back and walked out of the room.

Mom shook her head and bit her lip. She silently cleared the dishes and turned on the water at the sink. I could tell she was sad. She moved in slow motion and wiped her hands on the dish towel too often.

I heard the TV being turned on in the den. I didn't know whether to stay or leave. Mom must have read my mind. "You can go, Edith," she said quietly. "It's all right."

I walked into the den, which was next to the kitchen. Daddy was watching the news. The new president's wife, Jackie Kennedy, was on. She looked terrific in her little box hat. The announcer said that she was going to have a baby next month, in December. Then we watched *Rawhide,* my favorite show. The best part about it was the good cowboy played by this actor named Clint Eastwood. He was really handsome. He reminded me of someone in Mrs. Vanderbuildt's class, but I couldn't remember who it was. Whoever it was had the same great upside-down V eyebrows.

Uh-Oh lasted the rest of the night. I read this story once where a guy gets locked in this room and the ceiling starts moving toward the floor. The whole top part of the room just starts getting lower and lower and the guy is going to get flattened and he can't breathe too well, either. Well, that's what Uh-Oh felt like—like it was so heavy I was going to get trapped and crushed by it. Mom went to bed and Dad watched more TV. I figured I might as well go to bed myself.

After I had gotten into my pajamas, I pulled out my cloth-covered notebook from underneath my bed. I keep all my secrets in this notebook. It has a blue-and-white cotton cover and all the pages are blank inside. Or were. A *lot* of pages are covered now with little notes to myself or songs I've made up. Tonight I wrote:

> If only I could arrest the Purple Sweater
> like Clint Eastwood arrests people! If only I
> could run Uh-Oh out of town!

Then I went to sleep.

The next day, Saturday, I decided to call up one

of my old friends, Amy Cohen, but she wasn't home. I wanted to call my new friend, Rita Martinez, who was in Mrs. Vanderbuildt's class with me, but I didn't have her number. When I looked it up, there must have been five million Martinezes in the phone book. Besides, Rita was probably off having fun with her four sisters. Rita had told me that she and her sisters *did* get into fights sometimes, and once they had thrown live chickens at one another at their uncle's farm in Mexico. But even that sounded like fun. Being an only child isn't so great sometimes.

So I put down the phone book and went out to the front porch where Daddy was reading the newspaper. His sweatshirt and jeans had drips and drabs of red paint on them.

"Hey, Daddy?"

Daddy looked up from his paper. "And what may I do for you, young lady?"

"Can we go to Echo Park?"

"I don't see why not. Go tell your mother," he said.

I found Mom from the waist down outside her clothes closet in the hall. The rest of her was leaning inside the closet, covered up by all her kooky outfits.

"Mom," I said. "Daddy's taking me to Echo Park, okay?"

"Do you like this—" Mom said, sort of muffled from the closet, "or this?" She burst out of her closet and held up a vest with a jillion beads on it in one

15

hand and a really strange yellow-and-gold skirt with little holes in it in the other.

I giggled. "They're okay, I guess, but isn't Halloween over?"

Mom laughed. "You *pisk*," she said. *Pisk* is Yiddish for "big mouth." "They're for folk dancing, silly. Echo Park, huh? Fine. Take your jacket."

I love Echo Park. The first thing you see when you get off the freeway and circle the lake is the little lighthouse and boat house where the paddleboats are kept. All around the lake are these tall, tall palm trees, and at one end great big lily pads that float in the water. Too bad it was winter, because when the lilies are in bloom, they look like the perfect home for fairies and elves. There are islands and bridges in Echo Park, and best of all, there are ducks.

"Oh, Daddy! I forgot!" I said as my father parked the car. "Bread for the ducks!"

"Tell you what," Daddy said. "I'll buy some popcorn so we'll *all* be happy."

We went into the little boat house and Daddy rented a paddleboat and bought the popcorn. The man who ran the boat house had too many teeth, but I let him help me climb into the paddleboat anyway. The paddleboat was dark green with a green-and-gray-striped awning. It smelled funny, but then, paddleboats always smelled funny.

"Where to, Captain?" Daddy said. He looked kind of scrunched in the little boat.

"To the bridge, I think," I said. "That's where the ducks are."

I listened to the *swish-swish-swish* of the water and the *clunk-clunk-clunk* of the paddles as we moved backward out of the dock and crossed the lake.

After we had steered underneath the bridge I said, "All right, Skipper, hand over the popcorn." I pulled my legs from the pedals and felt the boat bob up and down. Some fat white ducks and a few little brown ones wiggled through the water toward the boat as Daddy and I tossed some popcorn their way. I took a breath and even looked around for a moment to see if any Purple Sweaters were hiding behind the palm trees.

"Daddy, can I ask you something?"

"Shoot."

"If . . . if one of these ducks was beating up one of the other ducks, but the other ducks didn't know it, what would you do?"

Daddy laughed and threw out another fistful of popcorn. "What would I do? I don't know if I could do anything, Edith. I don't talk to ducks as a general rule."

"No, really, Daddy—"

"Well, I suppose if there was a mean duck in the lake, someone from the parks department would take him out and keep him away from the other ducks. Why? Do you see a mean duck out there? They all look pretty happy to me."

This wasn't working at all. I sank down in my seat and let my arm dangle over the side of the boat. I felt the cool water pass between my fingers. Then I sat back up and tried again.

"Okay, how about this. Let's say you heard a rumor somewhere that there's some kid who's really different from everyone and there's another kid who doesn't like this first kid for being so different. So the second kid gives the first kid a hard time—you know, picks on her for not being the same."

Daddy looked at me as if I had just arrived from outer space. "What are you trying to say, Edith?"

I stared into the near-empty popcorn bag. Out of the corner of my eye, I could see the ducks shimmy away through the water. "I mean this girl can't do anything about being different so she really can't get away from this other person." I looked up and watched the ducks waddle up one of the islands. "I'm kind of a friend to this girl and she's sort of waiting for my advice and I don't know what to tell her."

"Well now," Daddy said, "first of all, you could tell her that if she needs a friend, Edith Gold is a good one to have—"

"Oh, Daddy—"

"And secondly, you could tell her that although

no one is exactly the same as anyone else, we're not all that different from one another, either. Maybe you could act as a go-between. You could help your friend and that other girl find out what they have in common. Then the three of you could be friends."

Oy marvelous. The Tree was right after all—no answer. "Thanks, Daddy," I said.

He smiled and ruffled my hair. "Sure," he said. "Anytime."

We didn't say anything more as we steered the boat back to the dock. Daddy looked so pleased with himself for giving me such great advice, I guess he figured that there was nothing more he could add. And me, I was at a *complete* loss.

On the way home, Daddy began to sing an old Russian folk song. His blue eyes always become bluer and more twinkly whenever he sings. His singing suddenly made me remember something—Monday was the Christmas chorus auditions! This was my answer! Starting Monday, I could escape the Purple Sweater and her gang! Chorus met a couple of times a week—maybe more—after school. I'd be off the playground for a long, long time and I'd be safe, safe, safe. Right?

Chapter Three

"YOU'RE loca if you think a pickle is gonna win over dot candy, Edith," Rita said at lunch on Monday. "Plain loca."

Every day, right after we ate our sandwiches, Rita Martinez and I would have a dessert contest. The rules were we had to have a different dessert every day of the week (I had thought of that one), the desserts had to look as good as they tasted (Rita's rule), and you had to be able to argue as to why your choice was the best. For some reason, Rita was usually the final judge, and for some reason, she also usually won.

Now Rita carefully wiped each of her fingers on her napkin and lifted this little flat package of folded Kleenex out of her lunch box. She opened up the package and unrolled a long white paper sprinkled with pale yellow, pink, and blue dots. They matched her yellow-and-pink ruffled dress perfectly.

"And they smell good, too," Rita said. She inhaled and batted her big, dark eyes. "Hmmmm!"

I unwrapped my giant kosher sour pickle from the wax paper. It *didn't* smell good, I had to admit that. But it *was* really huge.

"This'll last," I said, "for hours and hours."

"So'll this," Rita said and daintily began licking off the dots one by one with her tongue. With Rita, dot candy *would* last hours and hours.

"Pickles are a good dessert when it's hot and you want to cool down," I insisted.

"Edith, this is November and pickles aren't dessert," Rita insisted back. "I mean, have you ever had a pickle for dessert?"

This was true. Rita had won again. Just to prove I didn't care, I took a big bite out of my pickle. It certainly was juicy.

Rita screwed up her tiny nose and pointed to my waist. "Ooh, Edith! It's all over your dress!" I looked down. A whole river of pickle juice had splattered the front of my white wool skirt. I could feel dampness on my slip. *Oy* marvelous.

"Oh, Rita, what'll I—"

"Come on," Rita said. "I'll help you wipe it up."

So we ran to the bathroom. Then one of those weird, slow-motion things happened that you usually only see in old creepy horror movies. There are two wooden doors to the girls' bathroom that stand side by side—one marked ENTRANCE and one marked EXIT. Just as I shoved open the swinging door marked ENTRANCE, I saw the Purple Sweater's back as she pushed through the EXIT door on her way out. My stomach dropped to the floor tiles for a second, but the Purple Sweater hadn't seen me. Whew! Meanwhile, Rita must have torn off fifty thousand paper towels.

"Hey, Rita—"

"Hay is for horses," Rita said.

"It's just pickle juice. Don't get carried away."

"Do you wanna be dry or not?" Rita asked with wads and wads of paper towels in each hand.

The bell rang. Rita dumped all the paper towels in the trash and ran outside to join our class in line. I was left to mop up my poor old skirt by myself. Believe me, if this had been *Rita's* dress . . . well, never mind. I caught up with my class just as they came down the hall.

"Children! Children!" Mrs. Vanderbuildt was warbling. "Let's go in like little ladies and gentlemen and settle down. Come on, please."

Mrs. Vanderbuildt had the desks in our room arranged in this upside-down U or, as Mrs. Vanderbuildt liked to call it, a horseshoe shape. I sat between The Cathys—Cathy Ray and Cathy Reyes. The class had tried calling them Cathy One and

Cathy Two, but that had gotten mixed up pretty quickly. And after one of them got her hair curled (Cathy Reyes?) and looked just like the other one (Cathy Ray? Reyes?), everybody just gave up and said The Cathys. The Cathys were okay, but they sometimes chitchatted with each other like I wasn't there in between.

I wished I sat next to Rita. But Rita *did* sit across the U from me and we could make faces at each other. Like rolling our eyes as Mrs. Vanderbuildt took out her little square-frame glasses and said, "Now, then, a few announcements that I forgot to read this morning."

Mrs. Vanderbuildt was always forgetting something. Rita had told me that last Open House Night, Mrs. Vanderbuildt forgot where she had parked her car. She had a whole bunch of parents and teachers looking for it when she remembered she had gotten a ride with Mrs. Sutton.

"I want to remind you again," Mrs. Vanderbuildt continued as she held up a school bulletin, "that Miss Hauser is having the Christmas chorus auditions today after school, at three-fifteen, in the auditorium. 'We need more chorus people to make the Christmas concert a success' it says here. Now let me see." Mrs. Vanderbuildt put an index finger on her lips and looked around the room. "Linda, Marianne, you should go. Edith, you should definitely go. And Nick, of course! You all have such lovely voices!"

This big kid named Nick jumped up with one hand over his heart and the other arm outstretched. "Ohhhh, no-no-no-NO! Not me-me-me-ME-me-me-me!" he sang. He sounded like a bad opera singer gurgling underwater. Everyone laughed, including Mrs. Vanderbuildt.

Mrs. Vanderbuildt shook her head. "Don't be silly, Nick, I should think singing in chorus would be delightful. I think you *all* should go. It's just a suggestion." Nick brushed his palm over the top of his thick black crew cut and sat down.

"The other important announcement," Mrs. Vanderbuildt read on, "is that some time next week—after Thanksgiving—I can't tell you when because it has to be a surprise—we're going to have a Take Cover Drill. This is when we all crouch down in the hall, with our heads covered, in case of an A-bomb attack. We've practiced it before."

Yeah. I had had Take Cover Drills in my old school. I hated them and I was kind of scared of them, too. If the Russians ever dropped The Bomb on Los Angeles, nothing was supposed to happen to you if you just plopped to the floor and stuck your head between your knees. I mean, who really believed that? The thing is, nobody ever *said* how scared they were or how stupid this was because if you *did*, then *you* were a dirty Russian Communist, too. And I *especially* never said anything, 'cause my father *was* from Russia, and some people would hate me just for *that*.

"Edith!" Mrs. Vanderbuildt's voice cut in to my thoughts. "You're drifting, dear. Open your math book to our word problems, please."

After the stupid word problems came science and after science came P.E. and after P.E. came art and then, at last, after about a million minutes, school was over and it was time for the chorus auditions.

"Rita!" I shouted as the bell rang. "Are you going to go out for chorus?"

Rita pulled on one of her hoop earrings and scrunched up her nose. "No, *chica*. I sing like Nick does. Besides, I always have to go home with my sisters. But good luck!"

"Yeah, hope so!" I hoped more than Rita could know.

There were a bunch of kids waiting outside the auditorium. Sybil Something—I forgot her last name—showed up from my class, but since she never spoke to anybody, I didn't go over and speak to her. I was so nervous and excited that I twisted and twisted one of the buttons on my jacket until it popped off. Suddenly, the auditorium doors opened and Miss Hauser herself waved everyone inside.

She was wearing a black leotard and skirt, black tights and ballet shoes. Her hair looked as if someone had cut it in the dark. I had only seen Miss Hauser once before. She had come into Mrs. Vanderbuildt's class to give us a lesson on rhythm and she had somehow managed to play the autoharp and bongo drums at the same time. Now she was lining us up in front of the piano and asking us to sing "Row, Row, Row Your Boat."

"I can sing pretty high," I told Miss Hauser when my turn came. I brushed my hair out of my face and tucked the loose ends into my braid. It's hard to sing with hairs in your mouth.

Miss Hauser narrowed her eyes. Her black eye makeup made her look like a cat.

"Rightee-o, Ericka—"

"Edith," I corrected.

"Edith, I mean. Start about here." She played a chord on the piano.

"Row, row, row your boat/Gently down the stream—"

"That's fine," Miss Hauser said. "Take off your jacket. Let's go higher." Her hands moved up on the piano.

I took off my jacket and sang "Row, row, row your boat/Gently down the stream/Merrily—"

"No kidding—you're a soprano, Edith. Big voice on a little girl." Miss Hauser pointed to the stage. "See those other girls on the back riser? Those are the altos. We need some more sopranos to fill in so why don't you go up to the last riser in the soprano

27

section and stand in front of that girl in the purple sweater."

I looked up and saw Zandra Kott grinning her mountain-lion grin at me. The Boxer was on her right and the Tall Girl was on her left. *Oy* marvelous! Why hadn't I seen them come in? I stood right where Miss Hauser had left me beside the piano, feeling as if someone had shaken me by the shoulders too many times. How could this have happened?

Miss Hauser clapped her hands. "Rightee-o, everyone. After I've auditioned you, just find your place in the section I've told you to go to. And, old chorus people, make room for our new members."

Kids I hadn't noticed before were shuffling around on the risers. So that was it. Zandra was already in chorus. From the grin on her face, she probably had been waiting for me to show up. That's why I hadn't seen her every day. I thought I had been lucky or careful but Zandra had just been in chorus!

"Come on, Ericka—I mean Edith. Gary—you boys talking over there. Everybody, take your places please."

I slowly walked toward the stage like I was going to my own hanging. The auditorium had never seemed so cold or the wood so polished before. I noticed the two sisters in Zandra's gang on the way up to the last riser in the soprano section. I made my way to the end of the row. I could feel the Purple Sweater right behind me.

"The first carol we're going to learn," Miss Hauser explained, "is 'Hark! the Herald Angels Sing.' Four verses in four parts."

I shuffled through the mimeographed pages I'd been given. I could still smell the ink on the sheets. All the soprano parts were marked "melody" except for a couple of lines here and there. I decided to learn the words. Memorizing would use up some of the time it would take Miss Hauser to teach the altos and basses and tenors their parts. Maybe if I concentrated real hard, I'd forget who was standing in back of me. The second verse of "Hark! the Herald Angels Sing" read:

> Christ, by high-est heav'n a-dored;
> Christ, the ev-er-last-ing Lord
> Late in time be-hold him come,
> Off-spring of the vir-gin's womb.
> Veiled in flesh the God-head see;
> Hail th'in-car-nate De-i-ty,
> Pleased as man with men to dwell,
> Jesus, our Em-man-u-el . . .

Oy. I didn't mind singing about a baby away in a manger, but I felt funny singing about Jesus as an ev-er-last-ing Lord and De-i-ty. I quickly looked at some of the other carols:

... And un·to cer·tain shep·herds
Brought ti·dings of the same,
How that in Beth·le·hem was born
The Son of God by name. . . .

. . . Christ the Sav·ior is born,
Christ the Savior is born . . .

. . . Outside the ha·ll the moon shines bright
The be·lls of Par·a·dise I hear them ring
De·not·ing our Sav·ior was born this night
And I love my Lord Je·sus a·bove an·y·thing . . .

"Okay, everyone, let's try the first four lines,"
Miss Hauser said. She walked back to the piano and
played with one hand while conducting us with the
other. "Not bad. Let's go on and do the whole first
verse. With some feeling this time, all right·ee?"

I began to sing: "Hark! the Herald Angels sing/
Glory to the newborn King/Peace on Earth and
mercy *ouch!*" Zandra had pinched my neck! I must
have jumped up nine feet. The whole song stopped.
A few kids gave me what·are·you·weird? looks and
Miss Hauser frowned and clapped her hands.

"What's going on there? Ericka! Do you have a
problem?"

My braid was yanked down so hard my roots hurt
and I felt four or five fingers poking me in the back.

"Uh . . . no," I said.

"Then stop horsing around," Miss Hauser said, plainly annoyed. "When I said sing with feeling, I meant for the song, not your own."

That brought on some giggling. "Dumb fifth grader," a soprano in the first row whispered loudly.

We sang the song through once more. Then Miss Hauser taught us two more carols. Meanwhile, the end of my braid was knotted into little balls, my heels stepped on, and my neck pinched again. Miss Hauser interrupted the tenor's solo in the last song to tell me to stop squirming.

"And now," Miss Hauser said, "let us sing through all of our carols we have learned today and try to fill the auditorium with resounding joy."

But, to me, no matter how loudly we sang, Zandra's low chuckle was the loudest sound in the room.

Chapter Four

"THAT settles it, Ericka, you're out. Do you hear me?"

Oy marvelous. If Monday's chorus wasn't bad enough, Wednesday's was just about to get worse.

"Miss Hauser, I—"

"I cannot possibly conduct some of the finest Christmas music ever written with you fussing and stomping and turning and squeaking like a monkey. You're wasting our valuable time here. Do you hear me?"

"Miss Hauser—"

"If I didn't need you as a soprano—and you're a good soprano—" Miss Hauser closed her black-lined eyes and sighed. "All rightee, listen. Just leave for today, have a nice Thanksgiving, and come back next week when you can settle down. Is that clear, Ericka?"

"Miss Hauser—"

"What."

"They—" I felt the bony knuckles of the Boxer press underneath my ribs. "This ... I mean ... my name is Edith," I said finally.

"Edith, then. Kindly leave and think about controlling yourself next week."

"But you don't—"

"Now."

I took a breath and stiffly began to make my way down the risers.

Miss Hauser clapped her hands. " 'Joy to the World,' " she snapped.

Everyone began to sing as if nothing had happened, but I could feel a hundred eyes watching me go. I had never, never, *never* been in trouble like this before. In my wildest dreams, I never would've imagined a teacher asking me to leave a class. I put back my song sheets on top of the piano, walked over to the door, and pushed it open. The hallway was full of late-afternoon sun. I heard the auditorium doors close behind me with a *click*. My shoulders, which had been up around my ears, suddenly fell down. For a second, I thought of going back to talk to Miss Hauser after chorus and telling her what was really going on. But then I got this picture of her giving Zandra and the gang some lecture and then—wham—I'd be back against that old back fence with the Purple Sweater ten thousand times madder at me than usual. Zandra had warned me to keep quiet and that was probably the best idea. I felt bad, but I felt a little relieved, too. The Purple Sweater had gotten me once again, it was true, but for right now, she was nowhere near me.

I ran across the yard to the Hopscotch Tree and placed my hand on the black knot with the hole in it. I closed my eyes and saw myself back in chorus, except that now, every time Zandra or any of her gang would try to touch me, I'd take my foot off a secret rope that ran under the risers, up the auditorium walls, and across the ceiling. This rope held up a huge black pot that would overturn and dump a flood of boiling water on Zandra's head. I could just imagine it now: a flick of my foot—the rope zooms forward—this gigantic iron kettle flops over—and Zandra's soaking and steaming from scalding water. What a joke! I saw someone on *Rawhide* do this once. *Couldn't I rig that up?* I tilted back my head. *No*, the Tree answered quickly, *of course not*.

"I didn't think so," I said out loud. There was something underneath my left shoe. It was a really long pod, shaped like a smile. I picked it up. "Thanks," I said.

"Edith, what are you doing?"

I whirled around and there was Rita staring at me.

35

"Hi, Rita! I didn't see you. Why are you here after school? Don't you usually go right home?" I asked.

"Yeah, but I have to go to the dentist. My uncle's gonna pick me up. What were you doing?"

I pretended to laugh. "Just talking to myself."

"Uh-uh," Rita said. She tugged at one of her earrings. "You were talking to the Tree. When you ran out of the upper-grade building, I waved to you but you didn't even see me. Then I watched you come over here and . . . I don't know . . . *listen* or something. Then I walked over and heard you say 'I didn't think so' and 'Thanks.' You always do that? Talk to trees?"

"No," I said. I could feel myself smiling too hard. "Just this one."

"Just this one? The Hopscotch Tree?" Rita sat down on the bench. "Why?"

Rita had this very serious look on her face, like the look she gets when she knows she knows the answer on a test but she has to concentrate to remember it. I could tell she wasn't going to make fun of me. She was really curious.

"You really want to know?" I asked.

Rita leaned forward. "Yeah."

"Well," I said, "when I first moved here, I didn't know anybody. School had already started—right before Halloween, remember?—and it seemed that everyone had friends already. And where I used to live, I could walk home and stay at a neighbor's until my mom could pick me up. But now I live too far away to do that so I have to stay after on the playground. And that's how I noticed the Hopscotch Tree. Because I had no one to talk to."

Rita pulled at her skirt. "It talked to you?"

I patted the Hopscotch Tree. "Well, not exactly. I mean it does, but in its own way. Every time I went by it, I always had the feeling that it was watching me, trying to help me. It's different than all the other trees, you know."

Rita nodded. "I know. It's so big, it's all by itself back here."

"Not just that. It's . . . it's special. I mean, it's listening to us right now."

Rita's Bambi-brown eyes looked scared. She looked up. "It is?"

"Uh-huh," I said, "and . . . but I think I've said enough. It's kind of a secret."

"Ooh, Edith," Rita whispered. "I can keep a secret! Cross my heart and hope to die!" She X-ed herself over her blouse pocket.

"But, Edith—"

"Yeah?"

Rita wagged a finger at the ground. "Why did you pick up the whatchamacallit—that piece of wood?"

"The pod?"

"Pod."

"Oh," I said. "It's for good luck. You know, in case I get in a real fix or something."

Rita screwed up her nose. "But you have to be able to talk to it, right? I mean, it's not just magic like that"—she snapped her fingers—"right?"

"Right," I said.

A beat-up red station wagon pulled up outside the school's back gate and honked its horn. Rita turned and waved to it. Then she stood up.

"That's my uncle. I gotta go. Listen, Edith." Rita took both my hands and let her eyes wander up the Tree as if she were seeing every twig for the first time. "I think the Hopscotch Tree is great."

The station wagon honked again. "Ooh," Rita said. She let go of my hands and half ran, half walked over to the back gate.

"Happy Thanksgiving!" she yelled over her shoulder as she got into the car.

"You, too!" I shouted as they drove away.

I heard a rustle of leaves behind me. I put my palm over the knot between the twisted trunk. I closed my eyes. *That's my friend,* I explained silently. *I can share you with one friend, right?* The Tree nodded in little jerky flutters. I felt good. I had never seen the Tree laugh before. *But what do I do about chorus? And Zandra getting me in even more trouble? And Miss Hauser, who thinks I'm the biggest jerk alive?* The Tree stopped fluttering and was still. *Oy* marvelous. What did I do now?

Chapter Five

"OH, Mom! You're not going like *that*, are you?"

I stood in the hall outside my parents' bedroom and watched Mom put on her Thanksgiving Day earrings. They were little hanging plastic brown turkeys. Mom was wearing a brown-and-orange plaid skirt and orange sweater with orange patent leather shoes. Did I forget to say there was a turkey pin, too? There was a turkey pin, too.

Mom put her hands on her hips. "So, Miss Fashion *Meyvn*"—*meyvn* means "expert"—"what's wrong with it?"

"Well, I mean, we all know it's Thanksgiving. You look like you're a commercial for it, or something."

Mom threw back her head and laughed. "I thought you said you liked me looking as if I were on TV. Besides, I've worn this outfit for a couple of Thanksgivings now. You loved it two years ago."

"Mom!" I reminded her. "Two years ago, I was eight."

Mom just smiled. "Ah, now I see. Well, if this be the case, go see what your father's doing about loading up the car. Maybe we can get to Abe and Shirley's on time for once."

I left the hall and crossed the living room to the side porch. Daddy was lifting the last of our patio chairs into the trunk of the car. His gray sweater had two flecks of black paint on one of the shoulders. He looked up.

"Did your mother send you to spy on me, *Dooshsheesh-ka*? Tell her mission accomplished."

I straightened the sash on my lavender dress. "Daddy, how do I look?" I asked..

"You look fine, sweetie, very pretty. You're wearing your hair down today? No braid?"

"Yeah, but I don't look too kooky, do I?"

"Kooky? What's kooky? You look like a princess."

"Oh, Daddy," I said happily. "You always say that." He did, too.

Mom appeared from around the back with a coat over one arm and two bags of dinner rolls in the other. Her turkey earrings bobbed when she spoke. "All set? Let's go!"

We climbed into the car and started off for the Kleins'.

"God rest ye mer-ry, gen-tle-men/Let noth-ing you dis-may!" I sang softly from the back seat. Then I remembered the rest of the words—stuff about Our Sav-ior and Satan's Power—so I hummed what was left of the tune.

"What's that you're humming, honey?" Mom asked from up front.

"Chorus. For the Christmas concert."

"How's that going, Edith? Is it fun?" I could see the back of Mom's head looking into the rearview mirror.

"Huh? Oh, it's okay. Fine," I answered. I mean, what was I supposed to say? "Yeah, it was great until I got kicked out?"

Time to change the subject. "Are you working tomorrow, Daddy?"

"How about if I don't?" he asked. "You don't have school tomorrow and we could—"

"What?" Mom shouted. "Why wouldn't you work on Friday? I'm working on Friday! My office doesn't close!"

We came to a stoplight. "Well," Daddy said qui-etly. "Some of the guys are taking off, so—"

"Mortgages on new houses don't get paid by 'tak-ing off,' " Mom said between her teeth.

I stared out of the window as the light turned green. Nothing like a little Uh-Oh on a holiday. And

I had started it. Why did I have to go and open my big mouth and ask about Daddy's work? I rolled down the window, hoping the Uh-Oh in the car would blow away in the cool Thanksgiving air. Nobody said a word as we turned a corner and bounced up the Kleins' cracked driveway.

I watched my parents give each other a we'll-talk-about-this-later look and then we all got out of the car.

The Kleins lived in this building that looked like a Mexican castle. They lived on one side, with an upstairs and a downstairs, and some other family lived on the other side. Shirley Klein and my mom had grown up together in Brooklyn, New York. "We're friends like *this*," they'd always say and both of them would hold up a hand and squeeze the index finger next to the middle finger. Abe Klein had driven my parents to the hospital on the night I was born, so they're my godparents, although Jews don't really have godparents. The only thing wrong with them was their kids: Stevie (who's a year younger than I), Stanley (four years old), and Stuart (three years old). Anyway, we always went over to the Kleins' for Thanksgiving and they always came over to our house for Chanukah. And, of course, my mom talked to Shirley on the phone about a thousand times a week.

Shirley's big bright blue Mexican door opened and

Abe Klein and his mother, old Annie Klein, came out to greet us. Abe Klein was almost bald although he was younger than Daddy. "Hey, youse guys, good to see ya," he said, slapping Daddy on the back. "How's it going? Got those extra chairs?"

Annie Klein was this tiny plump lady with a lot of gold teeth and a strong Yiddish accent. She held my face in her hands and smooshed my cheeks together. *"A sheyn meydl!"* she said. That means "pretty girl." Old ladies always push your face together and then say how nice you look. I used to really hate it, but now it's okay, even though it's still not delightful. Daddy and Abe unloaded the chairs and we all went inside.

Stuart and Stanley were running around the living-room carpet like little weasels. Old Moe Klein, Abe's father, was on the couch, trying to light his pipe. "Simmer down, boys," he kept saying, "simmer down." I waved hello to Moe and zigzagged my way past Stuart and Stanley to the kitchen.

I don't remember anything ever smelling as juicy or as sweet or as spicy as that kitchen. Shirley whirled around when she saw me. She's the only person I know with freckles and red hair.

"*Bubele!* Happy Thanksgiving! I'm slaving away in here, would you believe? So what else is new?"

"Hi, Shirley," I said.

"So kiss me already, but don't touch. I'm sticky

43

with stuffing and flour and who knows what. Well! Get a load of you and how long your hair is! Got any boyfriends?"

"Shirl, she's only ten," Mom called out from the living room.

Shirley poked her head out of the kitchen. "Didn't stop *me*," she said, giggling. "Love those earrings, hon." Then she wiped her hands on her apron and went to talk with Mom.

The back door burst open and redheaded Stevie slammed the door behind him. "Are we eating yet? I'm starved," he yelled. "Oh, hiya, Edith."

"Hi."

"How's school? You having Drop Drills yet?"

"Not yet. Next week. Have you?"

"Yeah. Boy, are they stupid. Watch out for cooties."

"Cooties?"

"Yeah. At my school, there's this guy with cooties and he gets you during Drop Drills and makes you—"

"Stevie!" Shirley said at the kitchen doorway. "There you are. Would you please, for the hundredth time, go wash up and get your brothers washed up and sit down? We're almost ready to eat."

"Wanna see me roll my eyeballs back into my brain?" Stevie shouted as he walked backward into the living room.

"Not really," I said. Now, *why* would I want a boyfriend?

44

After everyone was rounded up, we all sat down to Thanksgiving dinner. The grown-ups were at the dining-room table while the Klein boys and I sat at this wobbly card table. It wasn't too bad because my parents sat at the end of the large table next to where I was. After Mom and Shirley had put out all the food, Moe Klein cleared his throat and brushed some of the pipe tobacco off his vest.

"To health," he said. The grown-ups lifted their wineglasses.

"We should all be thankful we are healthy," Annie Klein repeated. She smiled one of her golden smiles.

Abe Klein clinked his glass against Daddy's. "And a chess game after dinner, you louse," he said and then he winked at me.

Shirley raised her glass above everyone else's. "To a successful demonstration tomorrow."

"What demonstration, Shirley?" Mom asked.

Shirley put down her glass and began to pass around a bowl of sweet potatoes. "Oh, a bunch of us are meeting downtown at City Hall in favor of school integration."

"You think it does any good?" Annie Klein asked.

"So why not try?" Shirley said. "Why not—Stuart Michael Klein, get that out of Edith's plate this instant!"

I looked down and found a chewed-up plastic red cowboy soaking in my salad bowl. Little Stuart and

Stanley must have thought this was *the* funniest thing ever because they started laughing so hard Stanley tipped his patio chair over backward, crash-landed, and started crying.

Annie Klein jumped up. "Darlink!" she gasped.

"Did you hurt yourself?" Abe asked. Stanley shook his head. "No? Serves you right, then."

Mom got up and took my bowl away. Meanwhile, Stevie had picked up his eyelids between his thumb and index fingers and was just about to turn them up over themselves. I moved my chair closer to the grown-up table.

Daddy plopped some turkey onto my plate. "Where were we?" he said. "Shirley's right, you know. Even if we think 'nothing I do is going to change anything,' we should still do what's right for ourselves. And, after all, you never know when you can affect someone. Sometimes just showing up can prove a point."

Shirley tore off a piece of her dinner roll. "So you're joining me tomorrow?"

"I have to work," Daddy said.

Mom stopped cutting her meat for a second.

Moe Klein raised a finger in the air. "The history of the Jews—" he began.

"*Oy vey iz mir*, he's going to start with *that*?" Abe whispered loudly across the table. Everyone laughed.

Moe Klein wagged his finger again. "—Is such that we are fighters for social justice. Look at our fight against Egypt to end our slavery and to earn our civil rights—that's Passover. And our fight against the Greeks for religious freedom—that's Chanukah. And—"

"Shirley Klein marching around L.A. City Hall— that's Thanksgiving," Shirley interrupted. "I'm not a giver-upper, that's all. *'Beser der soyne zol bay mir guts zen, eyder ikh bay im shlekhts.'* "

"That's true," Mom said.

I shot a look to Mom, since I didn't understand *any* of this Yiddish, but she didn't look up.

Shirley smiled. "Eat up, everyone."

After dinner, Daddy and Abe played chess while the rest of us watched a Thanksgiving Day program on TV. There was a lot of singing and a stupid skit about Pilgrims and Indians. The end of it was interrupted by a special news report. Mrs. Kennedy had been rushed to the hospital and had given birth to a baby boy. Daddy made jokes about babies and the White House. Pretty soon it was time to leave. I watched for Uh-Oh creeping across my parents' faces as they got into their coats, but it seemed to have disappeared.

"Thank you! It was delicious as usual! See you at Chanukah!" Mom called out as Daddy and Abe loaded the patio chairs back into our car.

"Good-bye! Good-bye!" Moe and Annie Klein waved from the front lawn.

"See you later, alligator," Stevie said.

"Yeah," I said. Then I went up to Shirley, who was standing at her door with a wooden spoon in her hand.

"Bye, Godmother," I said as I kissed her good night.

"Bye, Godchild. See you soon, yes?"

"Shirley?" I asked. "What did you say in Yiddish at the table? You know, when you were talking about marching around City Hall?"

"Oh, you mean *'Beser der soyne zol bay mir—'* "

"Yeah. What's that mean?"

Shirley closed her eyes to translate. She's got freckles on her eyelids, too. " 'Better that my enemy should see good in me than I should see evil in him.' Why? You need the advice or you're just collecting Yiddish proverbs?"

"Uh . . . both," I said. "Thanks. Good night!"

As I rode home, I thought about what Shirley had said. It sounded great, but how would that stop someone from beating me up? I didn't know it then, but I was just about to receive an answer.

Chapter Six

WE could tell that something was going on by the expression on Mrs. Vanderbuildt's face. She had just finished reading the note some monitor on a hall pass had given her. She looked sort of startled. It was the same look she got when someone had to remind her what day of the week this was.

Mrs. Vanderbuildt cleared her throat. "Boys and girls," she announced. "It seems we have a change of plans for P.E. today. We're to play softball against Mrs. Sutton's class."

Mrs. Sutton's class!

Every single one of us groaned. Nick pushed back his chair, stood up, twirled around three times, and fell on the floor in a pretend faint. Nobody laughed. This wasn't funny.

The biggest and meanest kids at Layton Street School were in Mrs. Sutton's class. Zandra and most of her gang were in that class. I could feel my stomach do a couple of little jumps.

"Now, now, children, what kind of attitude is this?" Mrs. Vanderbuildt asked, but she sounded as if she were scared of Mrs. Sutton's class, too.

Nick got up off the floor. "Do I *have* to be captain?" he whined.

"Well, dear," Mrs. Vanderbuildt said. "You *are* the largest child our side has to offer. Now line up, everyone, please."

We all shuffled over to the door. Rita came up behind me and whispered, "We're gonna get killed."

"No kidding," I whispered back.

I wondered if Zandra would just grab the bat and swing it at my head in front of everybody.

Mrs. Sutton and her class were waiting in front of the Softball Tree when we arrived. I quickly spotted the Purple Sweater talking to the Boxer and some other girl in line. They were all looking at something the other girl had in her hand, so none of them looked up. Then I watched as Mrs. Sutton walked over to Mrs. Vanderbuildt. Mrs. Sutton looked perfect, as usual. She had this short blond flip that shone like a helmet in the sun and she always dressed like Jackie Kennedy. Today she was wearing a pale green suit with pale green high heels and a little gold bracelet. Mrs. Sutton would never ever be caught wearing turkey earrings.

"Thanks ssso, ssso much, Arlene," Mrs. Sutton said in her radio-commercial voice with lots of long S's. "You just sssaved me." Then she glided back across the playground to the upper-grade building and went inside.

Mrs. Vanderbuildt turned to both classes and clapped her hands. "Now then—" she began.

"We're up first. Mrs. Sutton said so," shouted "Rhino" Raymond. "Rhino" had a bump between his tiny eyes and a personality to go with his name. He was a team captain, too.

"Oh! Well! Certainly!" Mrs. Vanderbuildt said. She sounded as if she were apologizing for our class even showing up to play.

Nick told all of us to cover the bases and get way, way out there since everyone in Mrs. Sutton's class could easily hit the ball into Kansas.

"We're gonna be out here forever," Rita moaned as we ran out into center field. "I mean, this is a *joke*."

It was hot, too. I felt sweaty. I picked up my braid to wipe off the back of my neck and squinted at home plate. It seemed a million miles from where Rita and I were, but I could still see the Purple Sweater, now tied around Zandra's waist, coming up to bat.

Nick pitched the ball. There was a loud *crack* as Zandra whacked the ball high into right field. Both Cathys and two boys scrambled to catch it. The Cathys smacked into each other, one boy fell, and the other managed to pick up the ball and throw it to third. Zandra had already run home. *Oy* marvelous.

"Great," I said. "Just great. Hey, Rita—"

"Hay is for horses."

"Yeah, I know—are you as hot as I am?"

"No," Rita said. She was staring at the next batter. "It's not that hot. Why are we playing Mrs. Sutton's class in the first place? Huh? Nobody ever wins against Mrs. Sutton's class. It's gonna take a miracle for us just to—" Suddenly Rita stopped and blinked at me. "Ooh, Edith!" she squealed, jumping up and down. "Edith! Edith! Go get some!"

"Go get some what?"

"Some bark—I mean pods—from the Hopscotch Tree! Go get us some luck!"

That *really* made me break out in a sweat. "Rita!" I said. "That's our secret! Remember?"

Rita wouldn't stop bouncing. "But, Edith! No one has to know! And you said it would help you! You know how to talk to it! Tell it we need help!"

"Well, stop jumping up and down, at least," I said. "The whole class will think you're crazy."

I turned to look behind me at the Hopscotch Tree. It seemed like a huge stalk of broccoli from this distance.

"Edith," Rita hissed. "We're so far out here in

Nowhere Land that nobody'll even see you if you run real quick."

That was true. And I knew Rita was right—we needed some good luck magic if we were even going to score just one point. But the Hopscotch Tree was my special friend. It would be like giving it away.

Rita knew what I was thinking. She jiggled my shoulder and then jabbed her index finger into her chest. "Cross my heart, Edith, I won't tell *any*one. Just run and get some pods for us!"

"Okay," I finally said.

I waited until someone from Mrs. Sutton's class hit another homer—which was about a three-second wait—and I ran off to the Hopscotch Tree.

I leapt around to the far side of the Tree so that no one could see me and rubbed my palm against the knot with the hole in it. I wiped the sweat off my forehead and closed my eyes. *Zandra's team always wins,* I said silently to the Tree. *Could we win—or at least score—this time?* I looked up. All the leaves were pointing down. I looked at my feet. There, right between my shoes, was a little pile of seed pods.

"Thank you, thank you, thank you," I whispered. "This is going to work!"

I couldn't hold them all, so I scooped half the pods into my skirt pocket. I wished for probably the zillionth time that girls were allowed to wear pants to school. Pants have better pockets.

I looked back out at the game. There must have been a fight going on because most of Mrs. Sutton's class was clustered around the Softball Tree and Mrs. Vanderbuildt was in the middle of them, flapping her arms like a sea gull. Our class was still hanging around on the field.

And they were all facing me.

"Hurry up with the luck!" Nick yelled across the yard. "Before we start playing again!"

I sped back to the softball diamond and ran around giving out a seed pod to everyone.

"Here," I said as I pressed a pod into each kid's palm, "we can score with this."

Nick grabbed my hand when I gave him his. "The Hopscotch Tree really talks to you?" he asked. My mouth dropped open.

Meanwhile, Mrs. Vanderbuildt had finally managed to separate and bench the two boys who had been fighting. "Back to your playing positions!" she shouted. "Let us continue the game!"

I returned to center field. "Thanks," I said to Rita in my best oy-marvelous tone. "Thanks a bunch for telling the whole world about our secret."

"Oh, don't worry," she said cheerfully. "Everybody'll love you when we win."

We watched as "Rhino" Raymond came up to bat.

"What's the score?" I asked.

"Six—nothing, guess who," Rita said.

I expected Nick to pitch a no-hitter, but something

even better happened. "Rhino" smashed the ball across left field and Leonard Mooner caught it. Now, Leonard Mooner's glasses were always falling off because one of his ears was slightly lower than the other and Leonard Mooner's shirts were always buttoned wrong. I mean, he was the most out-of-it kid in the whole fifth grade and he caught "Rhino" Raymond's bomber ball as if he were a major leaguer or something!

"Wow! Did you see that?" I said.

"*Dios mío!*" Rita agreed.

The Tall Girl came up to bat and both Cathys— together—tagged her on her way to first. When the Boxer stood up to hit, she struck out.

We were up!

"Yay-ee-ee!" we all screamed and rushed for home plate. Mrs. Sutton's class rumbled past us on their way out to the field and I could see a few of them whispering among themselves and staring at me. I had this queasy feeling that they knew why we had a change of luck. Zandra looked as if she were going to come over and say something so I quickly moved next to Mrs. Vanderbuildt at the bench. Zandra glared at me for a second, grinned, and then ran off to cover first base.

Mrs. Vanderbuildt looked down at me sitting beside her. "Are you all right, dear?" she asked. "You look awfully pale."

Rita leaned across my lap and looked up at Mrs.

Vanderbuildt. "Edith's just excited," she explained, patting my knee, "because we're going to win. The Hopscotch Tree said so."

"Rita!" I said.

Mrs. Vanderbuildt looked confused. "The Hopscotch Tree what?"

Crack! Nick hit the ball out into center field and it got him to third because the two boys who had been fighting started up again when one of them dropped the ball.

We started to score. By the time I got up to bat, the bases were loaded and it was six–three.

"Edith will be our last batter," Mrs. Vanderbuildt shouted at the field. She pointed to her watch. "We're almost out of time."

I rose from the bench. As I picked the bat off the ground, I realized my hands were clammy and that my eyes hurt. My whole head was throbbing. Was I that jittery or was it something else?

I could see the Hopscotch Tree way behind "Rhino" Raymond's head. All the branches were moving in slow motion—up . . . and . . . down . . . and . . . up . . . and . . . down. . . . What was it trying to tell me? Slow . . . slow—go slow? Don't hit the ball too soon like I usually do?

"You ready or what?" "Rhino" Raymond grunted.

"Ready," I said, and swung the bat over my left shoulder.

I was hoping to hit the ball hard enough to at

least make it to second. I didn't want to get stuck at first base. Even out of the corner of my eye, I could see the Purple Sweater crouched and waiting for me.

"Rhino" threw in the ball and I made myself hold back until I couldn't stand it anymore and—*boom!*—the bat bashed the ball clear across the yard.

I had never hit a home run before in my life.

"Don't just stand there! Run, Edith, run!" my class was shouting. The kids on second and third base were already running home. I took off for first base.

Zandra had her arms out to grab me. "Hey, kike," she growled. "You think you—"

I didn't hear the rest. I dodged Zandra's claws, tapped the base, and ran for second.

"Throw it in here!" "Rhino" was shouting.

By the time I got to second, I was gulping for air. Over at home plate, my whole class was standing up, waving their seed pods over their heads and screaming.

I galloped to third base just as the ball was thrown into "Rhino" Raymond's mitt. Then I did something truly crazy and wonderful. I ran to home plate.

"Hey!" "Rhino" complained. "Stealing bases! Not fair! Hey!"

All the kids in my class gathered around me and slapped me on the back a couple million times.

"We won! We won!"

"Thanks to Edith!"

"Lucky pods!"

"We beat 'em!"

"Ooh, Edith," Rita said. "That was terrific!"

"Just like the Pirates over the Yankees in the World Series," Nick shouted. "Won by a run!"

Mrs. Vanderbuildt pulled a whistle out from somewhere and blew it. "Line up, children! We have to go in."

Mrs. Sutton's class slouched across the softball diamond and lined up next to us. Zandra stood next to me. Her eyes shone like wet green stones.

"Just wait till I get you in chorus today," she said quietly.

"I'm not going to chorus," I answered. My voice sounded as if it were coming from someone else and suddenly I knew why I had been feeling so hot. I slipped out of line and went up to my teacher.

"Mrs. Vanderbuildt?" I said.

Mrs. Vanderbuildt smiled down at me. "Yes, Edith?"

I knew I would have to say this next part real fast or I wouldn't be able to say it at all.

"I think I'm going to be sick."

Chapter Seven

MY eyes were closed but I knew I was awake. I knew because I could feel my flannel night-gown tucked up under my legs and the soft edge of the sheets tickling my nose. I took a deep breath, spread my arms up over my head, and stretched out my legs so that my toes touched the far end of the bed. That's when I realized I wasn't sick anymore. The achiness was gone. *Oy*, was this better than yesterday afternoon! All I had wanted to do (*after* I had thrown up in the nurse's trash can) was sink through the linoleum squares of the floor. But, in-stead, I lay burning up on that stupid, hard, scratchy bed in the nurse's office while I waited for Mom to come and get me.

Now, I touched my hands to my forehead. No

fever. I opened my eyes. Even though it was twi-light, I could still make out the brown shapes of my bookshelf, dollhouse, and dresser. There were two doors to my room. One led to the hallway and living room, while the other, on the opposite wall, led to the kitchen. I could hear sizzling and some thumping around from behind the door that led to the kitchen. Mom was cooking dinner. Wow, I must have been sleeping a long, long, time.

The only great thing about being sick (besides not going to school) was being waited on. I mean, I was probably perfectly able to go get something to eat, but it was a lot more fun to be served stuff in bed.

"Mom?" I said, but no one heard me because just at that second the phone rang.

"Can you get that?" Daddy shouted from the living room.

"Yes!" Mom whispered loudly from the kitchen. "But keep it down! Don't wake Edith!" The ringing phone was picked up.

"Hello? Oh, hi, Shirley, long time no hear, what's new?"

Well, maybe it would be better just to get up, after all. Talking to Shirley Klein was going to take about a million years. Mom had once burned a whole chicken while talking to Shirley Klein. I threw off my blankets, swung my legs over the bed, and stood up. I was a little dizzy, but okay. I walked over to the door that led to the kitchen and pushed it open a half inch.

"—and then an interesting thing happened when I went to go pick her up," Mom was saying. "There was another mother there and we got to talking."

Oh, yeah, I remembered that. I had been lying sideways on that marvelous bed, staring past the linoleum, at these two pairs of talking shoes. One pair of legs and blue heels had belonged to Mom and the other pair of legs had been plump, the feet stuffed into ugly brown loafers. I hadn't paid any attention to the shoes' conversation, though. In fact, I must have drifted off to sleep because I also remembered Mom gently waking me up and telling me we could go home.

"They just moved here from Chicago a few months ago," Mom went on, "and her daughter is having a rough time of it. She's fighting a lot at home and not doing well at school. Her mother says she's gotten in with a rough bunch of girls." Mom must have flipped something over in the pan because the sizzling was suddenly louder.

"Well, that's part of the problem. This girl did so poorly last year, she's been held back. You know, still in the fifth grade although she's quite old enough for sixth. That's why her mother was there. She had just had some meeting with the principal and her daughter's teacher."

Was that Mrs. Sutton? Some of the kids in Mrs. Sutton's class were held back. Was that the reason Mrs. Sutton had left her class with ours for P.E.? I quickly stepped back as Mom walked toward the bedroom door. The door was carefully closed. I waited until I heard a kitchen drawer slam and then I nudged the door open again.

"Wait, Shirley, let me just untangle the cord. There. I just wanted to shut Edith's door. My sweetie has been sleeping practically the whole day. Oh, she's fine. Fever broke this afternoon. Flu, you know. Nurse told me it's going around. So, anyway, this woman sees my Jewish star—oh, you know, Shirl, my little silver Jewish star? I wear it all the time. Yes, you do. Anyway—oh, wait."

There were three clicks as a burner on the stove was turned off. Something was burning. Something with onions. I wrinkled my nose.

"Almost lost it," Mom muttered. I couldn't tell if Mom was talking to herself or to Shirley. A chair scraped the kitchen floor.

"Let me just sit for a second so I can talk," Mom said. "So she sees my necklace and she says, very timidly, 'Are you Jewish?' I nod. 'Oh,' she says, 'so am I! My husband—my *ex*-husband's not—he's still back in Chicago—' She says, 'You know, Zandra hates being half Jewish; I don't know what it is with her—' Then, Shirl, she—out of the blue—she starts in with 'Oh, Zandra hates everything about me! Everything, everything, everything! I told her her father isn't so perfect either, you know? Ha ha ha!' Then she shakes her head and wipes *tears* from her eyes! She goes on and on about the divorce and moving to L.A. and Zandra's fighting and after what seemed like an hour she *finally* left. I felt sorry for her, but it was odd, Shirley, don't you think? The mother, I mean. Yes, exactly. Either crazy, or a drinker? Who knows! The poor girl, too. No, 'Zandra.' With a 'Z.' I know, it's an unusual name."

I dropped to my knees and my mouth fell open. What was going on here!?

"Oh, that's a good idea, Shirl." Mom was getting real chatty now. "I could have mentioned the Vermont Avenue Jewish Center, now, why didn't I? That poor girl certainly could use some help. Speaking of the Jewish Center, have you seen their horrible new Chanukah cards—?"

Poor girl?! Zandra?! The Purple Sweater could use some *help*??? The girl beats me up almost every day because I'm Jewish and now *she's* Jewish, too?! *What* was going on here?

I whirled around on my knees and my eyes must have darted around to every single object in my room. I had never seen the tiny couches in my dollhouse so clearly. I could almost touch the clay menorah on the bookshelf with my eyeballs. I could have burned the knobs off my dresser if I had stared hard enough. What was going on here? I knew what was going on here—I was mad. No, I was more than mad. I was . . . furious. *Furious.* How dare Zandra do this to me? I reached under my bed and pulled out my cloth-covered notebook. I couldn't really see what I was writing but I jabbed the pencil into the paper anyway. I wrote:

> I hate you I hate you I hate you!!!!!!!!!!!!!!
> I hate you for hating me!!!!!!!!!!!!!!!!!!!!!!!!
> <u>We are the same!</u>

I didn't know what else to write for a second so I just sat there and closed my eyes. I saw the top part of the Hopscotch Tree waving to me. Seeing the Hopscotch Tree when I closed my eyes wasn't unusual. Sometimes just before I went to sleep at night, I would imagine the Hopscotch Tree standing alone in the empty playground with only the stars around it. But this time it was daylight and the Tree's branches were reaching toward me and then folding back. Come closer, come closer, it seemed to say. I opened my eyes and looked back down at what I had written. After <u>We are the same!</u> I wrote:

> But we are <u>not</u> the same.
> I've got magic and you don't.
> There's no magic inside you if you're mean.

My door that led to the living room opened and I heard Daddy whisper "Edith?"

Time to hide the secret. I shut my notebook and pushed it back underneath the bed. I made myself smile in the dark.

"Hi, Daddy," I said.

Daddy snapped on the overhead lamp. "What are you doing sitting on the floor? You must be feeling better if you're sitting on the floor, yes?" he gently asked me.

"Yes," I agreed.

"Look," Daddy said as he walked over and helped me up, "your mother is still gabbing on the phone." Daddy opened and shut his fingers like a quacking duck. "So what do you say we just eat already—if there's anything not burned to a crisp—and she can catch up later. Are you hungry?" I nodded. Daddy smiled and laid the back of his paint-sprinkled hand on my forehead. "A good sign. Sometimes I think Shirley Klein phones up your mother at suppertime on purpose just so our meal will be ruined and we'll all think Shirley's a better cook than she really is."

I grinned.

As we walked into the kitchen, I felt as if something had shifted inside my chest. Zandra's secret was like a red-hot coal burning inside me. I could feel it glowing and keeping me warm as we sat down at the table to eat.

Chapter Eight

"EVERYBODY'S been waiting for you to get back!" Rita told me as we lined up for class Friday morning. She was right. Between spelling and math, I received four notes asking me to get some more magic from the Hopscotch Tree. At the first recess, kids were coming over and asking me if we really beat Mrs. Sutton's class because of the Hopscotch Tree.

By lunch, I had a whole crowd around me. I felt kind of embarrassed and silly trying to eat my sandwich and answer all these questions from kids I didn't even know. They were all squirming around the lunch table and hanging on to every word.

"Just pretend you're on TV," Rita whispered. She didn't seem a bit upset that we weren't going to be able to have our dessert contest. She just grinned and ate her lunch and told everybody that she was "there when the magic happened" and that if anybody wanted to speak to me, they would have to wait their turn.

"Next," Rita said, and pointed to a pudgy boy who I think was in the third grade. Half his lunch was on his shirt.

"What makes it magic, huh?" he asked. "And how come you're the only one who can get some?"

"I really don't know," I said. "I never even thought this out before. All I know is that it works for me."

"Next," Rita said in a teacher voice.

A girl who looked as if she cried a lot raised her hand. "Go ahead," Rita said.

"Does it give you things?" she asked.

I thought about that for a second. "No, I don't think so. It's more like a friend. It's hard to explain, but—"

"Well, what *does* it do?" said a really tall, pretty girl who I knew was in chorus. She had this wonderful wavy brown hair that didn't know what a knot was. She was in the sixth grade and I had always wanted to meet her. I knew she would never be my friend now since Miss Hauser had kicked me out of chorus. "I mean, if you're not sure why it works or what it does—" She rolled her eyes and shook her head.

Rita put down a French fry. "Hey," she said. "You just won't get any, all right?"

"*Rita,*" I said. "Please. Look," I said to the girl, "why don't you come after school and—" The bell rang.

"Why don't you all come to the Hopscotch Tree after school?" I continued. Most of the kids nodded at me before they threw away their milk cartons into the trash cans and ran across the yard to line up.

Rita carefully folded her napkin into a little square and put it back inside her lunch box. "What are you going to do at the Hopscotch Tree after school, Edith?"

I looked down at my bag of Fritos I hadn't gotten to eat. "I don't know," I said. "I guess I'll tell the Tree what's going on."

When we went back to class, Mrs. Vanderbuildt remembered the art project she had been meaning to tell us about that morning.

"Now that it's December and Christmas is coming, we're all going to make little angels with aluminum foil halos and wings." She clapped her hands. "Won't that be fun?"

I didn't think it would be all that much fun. It kind of reminded me of those words in the Christmas carols—all that stuff about the Son of God and Saviors. I cut out my angel along with the rest of the class but I felt apart from everyone while I was doing it. The two Cathys on either side of me were talking about what angels eat. Boy, it was sure easier being Jewish at home than in Layton Street School. I suddenly remembered then that I wasn't the only one—and I got hot and mad at myself for even thinking about Zandra. I cut her out of my thoughts as I sliced my scissors in a straight line through the cardboard.

RI-nnnnnnnnnnnnG! We all jumped. *RI-nnnn-nnnnnnnnG!* There was a few seconds of silence, and then the ringing repeated.

"Children! Children! That's our Take Cover Drill! It's here, so let's get prepared now!" Mrs. Vanderbuildt said. She turned chalk-white and her hands were fluttering.

We had each been assigned a place in line especially for these drills, but nobody remembered where. Mrs. Vanderbuildt marched us into the hall anyway.

Every time my parents talked about The Bomb, they spoke in Yiddish or spelled out half the words so that I wouldn't understand. I guess they didn't want me to know what they were talking about, but I knew anyway.

Sometimes when my parents had company over, like Abe and Shirley Klein or other friends, I would wake up late at night and I would hear them arguing about bomb shelters and the Cold War. It was as if there was this big Uh-Oh feeling all over America that any day now the U.S. was going to be attacked—we weren't *fighting* anybody—just that we were sort of waiting and, well, *suspicious*. I had asked my father what the Cold War was. He had shown me a map of Europe and said that it had something to do with an Iron Curtain on some countries and that it was stupid. But I knew that it was *not* stupid—it was serious. The Cold War was *so* serious that when we talked about current events in class, the Cold War was never mentioned. So kids had to find out about all this creepy stuff on their own.

"Duck and cover! Duck and cover!" Mrs. Vanderbuildt was shouting. We all crouched down facing the walls, heads tucked under our hands. All the other classes were doing this, too. I ended up squished between Nick on one side and Leonard Mooner on the other. Leonard Mooner closed his eyes as if he were going to take a nap. All the teachers walked around shushing us and telling us to be quiet during the drill.

Nick nudged me with his elbow. "Hey, Edith."

"Hey, yourself," I whispered back.

"I want some Hopscotch Tree magic right now," he said.

"It doesn't work like that," I said.

"Hey, *I* sent you two of those notes. I should get something," he said.

"Children!" Mrs. Vanderbuildt warned. She wagged her finger at us as she went by.

"Make something appear, like a brontosaurus." Nick knew a lot about dinosaurs.

"It doesn't work like that," I repeated. "Besides, a dinosaur wouldn't fit in here."

"Okay, a fighter plane, then." Nick's notebook was covered with fighter planes he had drawn.

"Still too big. And I don't think it gives you things," I said.

Leonard Mooner opened his eyes. "How about a white rabbit—like the kind out of a hat?" he asked.

Miss Hauser and the principal walked by.

"I'll try," I whispered. "Now be quiet." I didn't want to get into trouble again. And the only way I could talk to the Hopscotch Tree was to close my eyes and concentrate. I was picturing the Tree and me standing with my hand on the black knot, when I heard giggling around the corner from where we were crouched. I opened my eyes. Kids were getting up and running to see what the commotion was.

"Now get back! All of you!" Mrs. Vanderbuildt screamed. "The all clear hasn't sounded! Get back!"

The laughing got louder and suddenly, at the end of the hallway, there it was—a rabbit!

A white, white, white, white rabbit.

Leonard Mooner gasped. "Wow," he said.

"Double wow," said Nick.

"I know that rabbit," I said. "It's from the kindergarten. It must have escaped."

The rabbit took this terrific leap that startled everyone and then just sat in our hall with its tiny pink nose moving like crazy. Mrs. Vanderbuildt pressed herself against a wall and stared at the rabbit as if it were a rat or something. Nick began to snicker.

"Maybe she's allergic," Leonard Mooner said.

All these teachers surrounded the rabbit and then cleared away when Mrs. Upton, the kindergarten teacher, arrived. Mrs. Upton is truly old but she can definitely grab a rabbit. She scooped it up as if it were some twitchy little pillow and trotted away. The all clear sounded.

"Thank heavens," Mrs. Vanderbuildt said, waving her hankie up and down. "Thank heavens."

By the time we got back inside the classroom, word had gotten out that the Hopscotch Tree had made the rabbit appear. Leonard Mooner told the story over and over to anybody who would listen. I had never seen him look so lively. And Nick kept winking at me every time I looked around the room. Since he sat right across from me, his winks were hard to avoid. I didn't mind it really, though I had to wonder how Nick could wink so much without getting a headache. Then I realized who Nick reminded me of—Clint Eastwood on *Rawhide*! Same eyebrows! I winked back.

After school I ran over to the Hopscotch Tree hoping to get there before anybody else did. But there were already a few kids sitting on the bench and hanging around. Two of them were even playing hopscotch, using the pods as markers. The sixth-grade girl was there and so was the girl who probably cried a lot. There were some kids missing who had said they'd be there and some new kids I hadn't seen before.

"I heard 'bout the rabbit," a little boy said. He was missing some upper and lower teeth and he looked a little like a Halloween pumpkin face when he smiled.

"Look," I said to everyone. "I've never done this before. I mean, I never thought that what I know about the Tree would do anything and I sure was never going to tell anybody." I could see Rita running across the playground to join us. She must have gotten out of going right home with her sisters.

"Anyway," I said, "it's really better if it's as quiet as possible. So can we just wait until most of the kids leave the yard? Also, it has to get a little darker."

A few kids moaned. The teary girl said she had to leave and so did a few others. But six stayed. Nobody asked me anything as we waited around for the playground to get quiet and the sunset to start. Even Rita just sat and silently ate her dessert. It was a candy necklace. I definitely would have lost the contest again.

I stood against the fence and hoped the Tree wouldn't mind all these kids knowing about it. But, then, maybe it wanted all this attention. After all, we did beat Mrs. Sutton's class and the rabbit did appear, even if it was the kindergarten rabbit.

Finally, when all I could see were a couple of boys playing handball and the windows on the upper-grade building turned gold from the sun, I stood on the bench and faced the Tree. I could tell it was listening.

"Hi," I said. "You probably know what's going on. I didn't get to talk to you after I got sick on Wednesday. Thanks for the game and the rabbit. You didn't have to do that." I pointed to the circle of kids at the bench. "These are my friends. I mean, I don't know any of their names"—the little boy laughed—"but they're my friends because they believe you're magic like I do, so I'm going to teach them how we talk, okay?" The Tree nodded to me. I jumped off the bench and put my hand on the knot with the hole in it.

I closed my eyes and thought about chorus and if I should go back. In my mind, I could see Zandra behind me and those Christmas carols in front of me. I opened my eyes and looked up. To my surprise, the Hopscotch Tree was waving yes.

"Boy," I said. "I didn't expect that."

"Expect what?" Rita asked.

"What are you doing?" said a girl all in pink wearing a retainer.

"I close my eyes and ask a question," I said. "I don't ask for things, and except for what happened

75

on Wednesday, I usually don't ask for favors. Then I open my eyes and look up and get the answer."

Everybody tilted back their heads to see through the branches and leaves of the Hopscotch Tree.

"I don't see no answers," said the little boy.

"You mean the way the branches are moving? I do," said the sixth-grade girl. "Was it saying yes?"

"Yeah, you're right," said another girl who was squinting through thick glasses. "It's nodding."

"Ooh, Edith, what'd you ask?" Rita said.

"That," I said to everyone, "is what you don't tell. Anyone can know the answer, but only you and the Tree know the question. That way, it's a secret and it's special."

"What if there's no wind and the branches don't blow or you don't get an answer?" the sixth-grade girl asked.

"Well, first of all, the Hopscotch Tree doesn't need any wind to talk to you. Look around—do you see any of the other trees waving? Do you feel any breeze blowing?" All the kids looked off over the playground and then back up at the Hopscotch Tree and mumbled how I was right. "If I don't get an answer, then I take some of the pods, here, on the ground, for good luck. Sometimes I can get an answer by just watching the Tree in my mind."

I lined everyone up to show them how to touch the middle knot and imagine their question and then look up. Finally I picked up some pods to hand out to everyone. I was giving one to the girl with the retainer when I saw the Purple Sweater and her gang galloping over from across the yard.

"Oh, no," I said under my breath. My heart began to pound so hard it sounded like one of Miss Hauser's rhythm drums.

"Hey, *EEE-dith!*" Zandra called out with the usual smirk in her voice. I could see the Boxer and the Tall Girl and the rest of the gang running behind her. "You think you can hide over there, you stupid little—" Zandra was shouting, then she stopped and stood still. Her gang caught up with her and they stopped, too.

"Who's *that?*" the girl with the thick glasses said behind me. I had been staring so hard at Zandra, I had completely forgotten there were six kids around me.

"Zandra Kott," I whispered.

"Mrs. Sutton's class," Rita added.

"Oh," someone said, but I couldn't tell if they knew what being in Mrs. Sutton's class meant or not.

Zandra motioned her gang to stay back and slowly walked over to the Hopscotch Tree.

Zandra's walking over reminded me of this *Rawhide* episode when this bad guy corners the good guy and thinks he has him all alone and then all these townspeople appear out of nowhere. I suddenly wished Mr. Nick-with-the-Clint-Eastwood-eyebrows were here.

Zandra stopped about two feet in front of me. She always seemed so huge to me, and she was still pretty big now. But the sixth-grade girl behind me was taller. I could tell because Zandra's mean green eyes kept darting around to everyone and she had to look up a little at the sixth-grade girl. Zandra folded her arms across her chest and rocked from side to side on her heels. I had never seen her look confused before.

"Hey, Edith," she said. "What are you guys doing?"

Some girl with a high squeaky voice said, "She's been showing us how the Hopscotch Tree—"

"Don't tell her!" Rita said.

"Yeah, don't tell her," the sixth-grade girl said.

Zandra suddenly pointed at me. "Just remember what I told you, Edith Gold! You'd better not shout, don'tcha dare hide, and"—she began to back away—"you'd better not come back to chorus."

"I'm coming back," I said, but it was hard to hear me because I kind of cleared my throat when I said it.

Zandra took a step forward. "You what?"

"I'm coming back," I said a little louder.

Zandra pointed both hands at me. "You do and I tell Miss Hauser your secret!" she shouted. She

78

walked backward to her gang with her arms like two arrows at me the whole time. Then she snapped her fingers and the Purple Sweater and her gang scattered across the playground.

"Who was that?" the little boy asked.

"Ooh, Edith," Rita said, tugging at an earring. "What happened at chorus? You didn't tell me. And what's your secret?"

That was a good question. I shook my head. "I honestly don't know what she's talking about," I said.

"She's just stuck on herself is all," said the sixth-grade girl. "Hey, it's getting late. I gotta go." She held up her pod and smiled. "See you Monday," she said.

Rita's family station wagon pulled up outside the gate and she said good-bye and left.

The other kids finally left, too. The little boy was the last to go. His mother came walking down the street in a housedress with her hair wrapped up in a towel shouting, "Where have you been? Where have you been?" He ran out to meet her and she smacked his behind as they walked away.

Just as I sat back down on the bench, I heard our Chevrolet's honk. As I ran out of the gate, I realized that even with Zandra pointing at me, my stomach hadn't been melted cheese. But what was she going to tell Miss Hauser?

Chapter Nine

NOTHING much happened over the weekend. My dad and I walked over to the Natural History Museum to see the stuffed elephants and bobcats and all, which I've seen about a billion times. The best part was eating lunch downstairs in the cafeteria.

Saturday night my parents went folk dancing. I think my mom was wearing something with acorns and pinecones on it. The baby-sitter and I tried not to notice.

Monday started out okay until Rita pulled out an artichoke and some butter at lunch and won the dessert contest again. I thought I'd beat Rita at her own game by bringing in some old Mexican rock candy my mom had bought at Olvera Street downtown, but even I had to admit that a boiled artichoke dipped in melted butter was terrific (even if it did look awfully like a pickle). I watched Rita dip her little finger into the tiny plastic butter bowl and then run her finger over her mouth as if she were putting on yellow lipstick.

"Ooh, Edith," she said. "Is Zandra gonna make trouble for you in chorus?"

"Yeah, probably," I said, although I still could not imagine what else Zandra could do.

Rita pressed her lips together. "You know, when I came to school this morning, I asked the Hopscotch Tree for some advice, and it said no. And I think it was right."

"What did you ask?" I said, but I was really thinking about Zandra.

"Oh, no you don't!" Rita gave me a little push off the bench. "That's my secret, remember?"

"Yeah, you're right," I said. "Sorry."

We went back to class and things sort of slid downhill. I was disappointed that Nick wasn't winking at me today. He seemed to have become best buddies with creepy Glen Knight. I didn't like Glen at all. He drew swastikas all over his notebook and said things like Kennedy shouldn't be president because he's a Catholic, which, in the first place, was a very stupid thing to say, and in the second place was especially stupid at Layton Street School where nearly everybody was Catholic or something like that. I hoped Nick's interest in Glen was only for today.

Then Mrs. Vanderbuildt insisted we do last week's spelling test again because everyone (not just me this time) did so badly. *That* certainly brightened up the afternoon. I thought again about not going back to chorus. But that would just be letting Zandra get her way completely. Besides, I hadn't done anything wrong, even though Miss Hauser didn't—and wouldn't—know it. The Hopscotch Tree was right—it was best to go back.

Miss Hauser was passing out more sheet music at the door when I got to the auditorium. She scrunched up her nose a little when she saw me. One of those quick little scrunches like when someone asks you if you like horseradish or not.

"You're going to have to catch up, Ericka," she said. She was wearing black again, including the black ballet shoes.

"That's okay! Really! That's okay!" I said, trying to sound like a character in a Disney movie—all chirpy and sweet. The Purple Sweater was there except that today her sweater was white. I tried not to look at her at all as we got onto the risers to sing. She must have told her gang not to bother me because nothing happened for about three songs. Then, just when I was beginning to think she'd forgotten about her threat, Zandra raised her hand after we'd sung "Down In Yon Forest."

"Miss Hauser? Miss Hauser?" Now *Zandra* sounded like a character from a Disney movie.

Miss Hauser was standing at the piano, one hand on the keys and the other hand on her hip, frowning down at the sheet music in front of her.

"Miss Hauser?"

Miss Hauser looked up. "Yes, Zandra?"

"I think you should know that Edith Gold is not singing all the words."

Oy marvelous. I felt my tongue jam up against my front teeth and my whole body temperature go up about two hundred degrees. The girls standing next to me moved away a little. Miss Hauser sighed loudly and walked over. The sixth-grade girl with the great hair, who was on the first riser, glanced back over her shoulder with a confused expression on her face. A lot of kids were staring at me.

Miss Hauser squinted up at the risers. "Ericka—uhm—Edith—is this true? You don't know the words?" She didn't sound that mad.

Zandra jumped right in. "Oh, it's not that she doesn't *know* the words, it's just that she refuses to sing *certain* words." Zandra was practically squealing. "I stand right behind her and I can see it's just certain words, the same ones, all the time, like—"

Miss Hauser motioned Zandra to stop. "That's enough, Zandra, I get the point. Edith? Are you having trouble with some of the words?"

"She won't sing 'I love my Lord Je-sus above any-thing,' " Zandra blurted out.

"All right, Zandra," Miss Hauser said impatiently. Somebody giggled at Zandra. Miss Hauser stepped closer to the risers. "Edith, is this true? You're not singing that?"

"No, I mean, yes. I mean, it's true," I said. My cheeks were as hot as toasted waffles.

"Why won't you sing certain lines?" Miss Hauser asked softly.

"Because—" My throat felt like a pencil was caught in it, going sideways. My waffle cheeks were now burning and wet. "Because I'm Jewish. And it's hard to sing those words. Sometimes."

Miss Hauser closed her eyes. "Oh," she said quietly. "See me after chorus, all rightee? And, Zandra?"

"Yes?"

"Mind your own business!"

Two of Zandra's gang laughed out loud. Zandra poked them in the ribs.

The rest of the rehearsal went smoothly. At four o'clock, everyone stepped off the stage, piled their music sheets on top of the piano, and went home. Zandra gave me this really smug boy-are-you-in-trouble look as she got to the door. She began whis-tling those stupid beginning lines to "Santa Claus Is Coming to Town."

I sat down on the riser. To my surprise, Miss

Hauser tucked up her black skirt and climbed up the risers to meet me. She looked tired and her black cat-eye makeup was cracked.

"I didn't realize you were Jewish, Edith," she said. "I'm afraid I'm not familiar with, uh, traditional Hebrew songs, or else—"

"That's okay," I said. "It's a Christmas concert. Besides, I celebrate Chanukah—"

"Oh, yes, Han-ook-ka." Miss Hauser pronounced it as if it were the name of a Japanese girl.

"Yeah, well, we celebrate it at home and at the Vermont Avenue Jewish Center, so—"

"But still," Miss Hauser said, taking my hand. "I don't want you to feel forced or . . . or . . . hurt in any way by singing these old English carols. You don't have to hide the fact that you're Jewish . . ." Miss Hauser's voice trailed off.

Hide that I was Jewish? I wasn't doing that, was I? *Zandra* did that, but I—

"Edith!" Miss Hauser suddenly brightened up. "What if you sang a solo?"

I blinked. "A solo?"

"Yes! You certainly have a good enough voice. Why don't you sing one of your Han-ook-ka songs— and bring in the music so I can play it for you—and you can sing it at the concert!"

I couldn't believe it. "You mean it? A solo?"

I suddenly felt that little hot coal of Zandra burn a little. "Uh, Miss Hauser?" I asked. "Could I . . . I mean, would it be all right to add a few words of my own at the end, in the song, I mean?"

"Sure, why not?" She wagged a finger at me. "Not too long now—I'm sure you could really ham it up if I let you."

Boy, did this afternoon turn out different! "Thanks, Miss Hauser! Thank you!" I said.

Miss Hauser stood up. "It's getting late. We'll try it out on Wednesday, all rightee?"

I grinned. "All rightee."

I could have flown out of the auditorium just by flapping my arms, I was so happy. I ran down the risers and skipped over to the door.

"Thanks, Miss Hauser!" I shouted. "You're cool!"

"You're welcome, Edith," Miss Hauser said, smiling. "See you Wednesday!"

I ran out of the building and was just about to head over to the Hopscotch Tree to tell it my good news when I saw my mom's car come down the block.

I watched as my mother pulled up to the back gate and parked. I could see that Mom was wearing her red jumper and white blouse with a red scarf circling her bun. Compared to Miss Hauser, Mom looked like a model. Well, maybe not a model— Mom would never dress like Mrs. Sutton did. But I realized, as I climbed into the car, that if Miss Hauser ever stopped wearing black, black, black, she'd be almost as beautiful as my mom.

Chapter Ten

"WELL," Mom said that night. "If you're going to sing just one Chanukah song at a Christmas concert, why don't you sing 'Chanukah, O Chanukah'?"

I rolled my eyes. "Oh, Mom. That's so old! And boring!"

We were sitting cross-legged on the floor of my room looking through some Chanukah song sheets that Mom had helped write down for a party a couple of years ago. I could hear the tinkle and chink of the dinner dishes being washed and Daddy's Russian humming coming from the kitchen.

"Besides," I added. "Everybody knows it."

Mom laughed and poked me in the shoulder. "No,

Edith! That's the point—*not* everybody knows it! Not at Layton Street School. Right?"

"Yeah," I admitted. "That's right. I guess if you've never heard it before . . ." Zandra's face lit up inside me and I wondered if *she* had ever heard the song before. Well, she sure was never going to hear it like *I* was going to sing it.

I took the "Chanukah, O Chanukah" sheet out from beneath the other songs. "Okay, Mom, you win. Besides, I get to write more words to it anyway."

Mom looked puzzled. "Why would you write more words—"

"Oh, because I get to, that's all." I tried to say this like it was no big deal and shuffled the other Chanukah songs into a pile. "Miss Hauser said I could. Here." I handed the rest of the song sheets to Mom. "I'd better start working on my own verse right away. Thanks a lot, Mom, really. Thanks."

Mom smiled. "Okay, okay, I get the hint I'm sup-posed to leave now." She stood up. "Have fun writ-ing that last verse."

"Oh, don't worry," I said. "I will."

As soon as Mom left, I got out my cloth-covered notebook from underneath my bed and looked again at what I had written on the night I had found out the Purple Sweater was Jewish:

I hate you I hate you I hate you!!!!!!!!!!!!!!!!!!!!!
I hate you for hating me!!!!!!!!!!!!!!!!!!!!!!!!!!!!!
<u>We are the same!</u>
But we are *not* the same.
I've got magic and you don't.
There's no magic inside you if you're mean.

I wanted to write a verse that had that in it. I wanted to let Zandra know that I knew her secret. Mom had to tell me to turn off the lights twice before I was finally through on Tuesday night.

Then, on Wednesday, chorus was canceled because Miss Hauser was sick or something.

I was a little scared about waiting after school because I knew Zandra hadn't gone to chorus either. I thought I did see her at one point. She was standing in this one ray of sun over by the upper-grade building. I was spinning around the Hopscotch Tree pretending to be a bird or a pirate or something and I remember seeing a faraway blur of purple and gold. She had been all by herself. When I stopped twirling, she was gone.

But Friday—Friday was a whole other horse of a different color altogether, as my mother would say.

The first thing Miss Hauser did was to move me down to the first riser and then announce to the whole chorus that I was going to sing a solo in the Christmas concert. I got this great look from the sixth-grade girl with the no-knots hair. She seemed real proud of me. But there was some shuffling around from the top riser where the Purple Sweater and her gang were standing.

"We won't hear your solo just yet, Edith," Miss Hauser said. "Let me take a look at it after rehearsal today." Then we went through the whole program. I even sang all the words.

After chorus, I went up to Miss Hauser's piano and showed her my song.

"It's lovely," Miss Hauser said, "but, Edith, I don't quite understand the last verse."

I knew she would say that. "It's a kind of message," I explained. "You know, like in a bottle or in a fortune cookie? I thought about it a lot. I must have written that verse over about a zillion times."

Miss Hauser smiled. "A zillion? All right, Edith. Sing it for me now and then we'll sing it again in chorus on Monday for our dress rehearsal. Tuesday's the show!"

I sang my song about three or four times with Miss Hauser giving me suggestions on pronunciation and projection and stuff like that. Finally, Miss Hauser told me I was just fine, patted me on the back, and left in the direction of the office. I looked up at the auditorium clock. I had told my mother to pick me up late, at five. It was almost ten to five now. I was sure that it was too late for the Purple Sweater and her gang to be still hanging around. I was wrong.

They had been standing behind the outside hall doors and I heard them as I went down the steps of the upper-grade building:

> "You'd better not shout,
>   Don'tcha dare hide,
>   You'd better watch out,
>   I'm telling you why,
>   Zandra Kott is gonna get you."

My stomach did that old melted cheese thing again except that this time it did it so fast my breath went with it. And I started to shake. Just like that.

"Hey, Jew girl," Zandra growled. One of her gang shoved me down the stairs. They all trotted after and surrounded me in this little circle as if I were a handball and they were the walls. Every time Zandra said something, the four girls would repeat what she had said and one of them would push me across to another, who would push me back again.

"So now you're singing solo," said the Purple Sweater.

"So now you're singing solo," the gang repeated after her. I was shoved across. Shoved back.

"You think you're better."

"You think you're better." Shove, shove.

"All kikes do," Zandra said.

"All kikes do," said the gang. Shove, shove.

I wished Nick were here. I wished Miss Hauser

were here. I wished Daddy were here. But most of all I wished that I were seven feet tall and really strong. I never wanted to hit someone so much in my life as I wanted to hit Zandra right then. But I felt like my body had disappeared.

"Jews stink," Zandra said.

"Jews stink," echoed the other girls. Shove.

I opened my mouth. "Does your mother stink, too, Zandra?"

I couldn't believe I had said that. From the look on her face, Zandra couldn't believe it either. For a second, the whole world was still.

Then I burst out of the circle and ran straight across the yard to the Hopscotch Tree. I hugged it so tight the bark hurt my arms. They were running after me. I closed my eyes, but then I heard them stop. When I opened my eyes, the Purple Sweater was waving her gang away.

"Don't go near the Hopscotch Tree," she shouted. "Haven't you heard about that Tree? It gives you bad luck. Yeah." Then Zandra reached down and picked something up from the yard—a rock or some glass—and threw it at me. It bounced off the Hopscotch Tree. Then they all ran away.

I pressed my cheek against the knot with the hole in it. It was warm, warmer than I was. *They were mean to me*, I said silently to the Tree. *Yes*, the Tree answered. *I liked being mean back*, I said. *Yes*, said the Tree. *But I don't really like being mean*, I said.

The branches and leaves swayed back and forth. *No,* the Tree agreed. *I have to find a way to make her stop, once and for all,* I said. *I have to make her listen. Can I do that by Tuesday?* I asked. The Tree was still. Then it began to wave *yes, yes, yes, yes, yes.*

Chapter Eleven

OKAY, I had decided, no more stories about ducks—I would tell my parents about the Purple Sweater at dinnertime. I never got the chance. When Daddy came home from work, the first thing he did was walk into the kitchen and say: "I got laid off."

Mom banged down the saucepan of peas a little too hard, turned off the lamb chops, and crossed her arms over her chest.

"You what?"

"I got laid off. Don't look at me like that. It's not my fault. All of us did. It's not such a crime. It happens."

"Why?" Mom wanted to know.

"Why, she asks." Daddy swung his old tin lunch pail up onto the counter and opened it. He took out an apple core and threw it into the garbage. "Because they ran out of money. Or so they claim. I think it's because they wanted to hire the landlord's son. Non-union."

"Non-union" was something you didn't say in our house. "Non-union" was like saying "I hate babies." Mom worked for a union. If you were in the union, everyone else in the union was your brother or sister.

Mom unfolded her arms and wiped her hands across her apron. "Wouldn't you know. Well," she said, sighing, "I don't know how we're going to get by."

"We'll get by," Daddy said. He began undoing the straps of his overalls. "We always do."

"On the back of my salary," Mom muttered. She snapped the lamb chops back on.

Daddy stopped fiddling with his overalls. "You're starting that again? I'll get another job," he said gruffly.

"And when will that be?" Mom folded her arms again. "It's almost the holidays! When? After New Year's? You know it's slow in winter! Nobody paints their house in winter!"

"That," Daddy said as if he had said this a hundred times before, which he had, "is the nature of the business. All contracting is like that."

"Then maybe it's time to find another business," Mom said. She had said this a hundred times before, too.

Uh-oh. Uh-oh. Another fight was starting. I hadn't even said anything this time.

Mom lit the Sabbath candles but her mood was pretty sad and dinner was very quiet. At first, I felt angry at my mom for yelling at Daddy just when he got laid off. Then I was angry at Daddy for not understanding Mom when she said she'd have to be the only one to support us. Then I didn't know what to feel. What if Dad didn't get another job? What would happen if *Mom* got laid off? How come I felt as if *I* had done something wrong? What would happen to us? The only thing good about dinner was that Mom said she was pleased that I ate every single pea on my plate. I didn't know what else to do, since nobody was talking to anybody.

After dinner, Daddy wanted to go folk dancing but Mom didn't. Mom went to bed early and Dad went to bed late. Marvelous.

Saturday morning was just the teensiest-weensiest better, but not much. Mom and Daddy didn't sound angry when they spoke to each other, just sort of sad and far away, as if they were both thinking of different things. It was still enough Uh-Oh for me to want to go away for a while. I decided to go up to the attic, which is not really an attic, it's this loft above our garage. And it's not as if I don't know every piece of junk in there, but ever since we moved, I do find something new, every once in a while.

So I left my house full of Uh-Oh and climbed up the dusty, squeaky stairs to the room above the garage where all my old baby stuff and my parents' New York boxes are stored. I usually just go through all my old toys—some stuffed animals, the rocking horse, the doll's cradle—and never bother with the New York boxes. They're mostly boring things like thick books in Russian (which don't turn into English even if you hold them upside down in front of a mirror) or train schedules and old newspapers. But then I saw this little box I hadn't opened in a long time. Once, I had found a calendar with a lady wearing ruffled shorts and a top and a lot of red, red lipstick on the cover. I had shown it to my parents and they had laughed and said the lady was What's-Her-Name who was really famous a long time ago. Anyway, I opened up the little box and found a lot of the old magazines and typewriter paper I already knew were there. But then this small brown envelope slipped out from one of the magazines. It was addressed to:

Miss Bender
Evergreen Lodge
Evergreen, New York

I opened the envelope and inside was a letter that read:

Darling—
Only work—mindless, slavish, and necessary work—drives me away from you! As I came in by train and then by subway, I watched the dull, unhappy faces of the working men and women who must leave their summer weekend retreats for the factories and offices of Manhattan. And I knew I was one of those unhappy toilers! Which only made me long for you all the more.

Do you miss me? When I close my eyes, I still see you dancing across the Evergreen stage, your warm smile and laughter lighting up the whole place. Do you love me? Do you remember our last night by the lake? I hope you do.

Katie called and told me you might come in next weekend. Let's hope I'm not working the Saturday shift! It's raining buckets right now—it really started pouring just as I got into my apartment—which means I'll have to start out early in order to get to work on time. My ceiling is already dripping a little. But all this is as insignificant as Hitler's mustache when I think of the two of us in the Evergreen moonlight. Got to run.

I love you,
Curly

P.S. Will you send me a letter tomorrow?

I didn't understand all the words, especially the part about Hitler's mustache, but I knew in an instant what this letter was. Daddy's nickname was Curly. Mom called him that sometimes when they were teasing each other or when they were all dressed up and about to go out. And Mom's last name before she was married was Bender. This was a love letter from my dad to my mom!

I stuffed the letter back into the envelope, ran downstairs, out into the yard, and tore open the back door of the house.

"Mom!" I yelled. "Mom!"

"My God, I'm right here, Edith!" Mom stood up from the living-room couch. Her hair was in a pony-tail and she was wearing pedal pushers, but she looked okay. She held her hand over her heart. "Don't scare me like that," she said. "What is it? Is something wrong?"

I shoved the letter into her hand. "Read this," I said. "What does 'toiler' mean?"

"It means someone who works really"—Mom's voice kind of faded out as she began to read the letter—"hard . . ." she said finally. But there was a big smile on her face. "Oh, my, oh, my," she said softly. "Where did you find this?"

"In the attic," I said. "It's from Daddy, right? When you guys were in love?"

Mom turned and walked over to the front porch

and pushed the screen door open a crack. "Could you come in here for a minute?" she said.

I could hear the rustle of Saturday's papers being put down and then Daddy walked in and stared at us. "What's going on?" he asked. I could tell he was still uncomfortable with Mom.

Mom handed him the letter. "Here," she said. "Remember?"

Daddy looked puzzled at first, but he, too, was smiling by the time he had finished reading. "What a year that was," he said half to himself.

"Edith asked if this was from you," Mom said to Dad. "When we were in love. How would you answer that, hon?"

Daddy put an arm around Mom's shoulder and gave her a squeeze. "We are still in love, Edith," Daddy said. "We just fight sometimes, that's all."

Mom pulled me to her. "Did you want us to stop fighting? Is that why you brought in the letter?"

"Yeah, I guess so," I said quietly.

"Not a bad idea," Daddy said. " 'A kindersher seykhl iz oykhet a seykhl.' 'A child's wisdom is also wisdom.' "

Mom gave Daddy a playful little poke with her elbow. Then she put her arms around my shoulders. "Edith," she said, "I know it's upsetting when your father and I fight. But sometimes we can't help it. Even people who love each other fight with each other. That's normal, okay?"

I must not have looked too happy with that because she added, "And you don't have to worry
about us when we fight."

"*Doosh-sheesh-ka,*" Daddy said slowly. "Our fights
have nothing to do with you. We're not mad at you.
And nothing bad is going to happen to you if we
fight."

"For that matter, nothing bad is going to happen
to you if *you* fight sometimes," Mom said. "As long
as you know what you're fighting for, then you don't
have to feel ashamed about it, okay?"

Then Mom gave me a big hug and Daddy gave
her a big hug and then we all laughed a little because
it was awkward getting out of a three-person hug.

On Sunday, Mom and I went Chanukah shopping
for Daddy and some friends. All the Christmas deco-
rations were up all over the stores. I don't mind the
blinking lights and the mistletoe, but I'll never get
used to the sprayed-on snow and plastic snowmen.
Not when there are palm trees in the parking lot
right outside.

Even Layton Street School had fake icicles and
tinsel on all the doors and windows Monday morning. Poor Mrs. Vanderbuildt tried to go through the
day wearing this stupid Santa's hat that kept swat-
ting her in the eye until she finally took it off. And
even Miss Hauser wore a tiny, tiny red-and-green
pin on her black leotard that afternoon.

We rehearsed the whole Christmas program as if it were the real performance. Some of the sixth graders had been given introductions to read before some of the songs. One or two of the introductions got messed up, but Miss Hauser didn't stop. She didn't even appear worried when the tenor section lost its place for a while in "What Child Is This?"

Just as we came to the end, she said, "Now that is what I call a professional dress rehearsal. Very good, boys and girls, very good. All rightee now, Edith? Shall we hear 'Han-ook-ka, O Han-ook-ka'?"

I stepped forward. I felt like I was going to go on a roller coaster—scared, but excited, but scared, but excited.

"Turn a little to your left, Edith," Miss Hauser said from the piano. "That's it. You're stronger on the diagonal."

I could see Zandra on the top riser just off my left shoulder. She was scowling.

Miss Hauser began to play the introduction. Then I began to sing:

> "O Chanukah, O Chanukah,
> Come light the menorah!
> Let's have a party,
> We'll all dance the hora!
> Gather 'round the table
> Let's have a treat

Dreidels to play with
Latkes to eat!

"And while we are playing
The candles are burning low:
One for each night
They shed a sweet light
To remind us of days long ago—oh!
One for each night
They shed a sweet light
To remind us of days long ago."

I sang the "O Chanukah, O Chanukah" part
again and then turned slightly toward Zandra for
the third, made-up verse. I stared straight at her.
She was looking away from me at that moment,
but I guess I was staring so hard at her that one
of her gang nudged her and the Purple Sweater
blinked back at me. I sang the last verse right to
her:

"If you sometimes wonder
If you like being a Jew,
Think why should you hide
The magic inside
That's there for me and for you—too!
Why should you hide

The magic inside
That's there for me and for you."

Miss Hauser gave a big finish on the piano. "Very
nice, Edith. Remember your pronunciation. And
stand up straight. And don't turn too much to the
left. Let's finish up with our last song and then
you're all dismissed until tomorrow! Remember—
white blouses for the girls and ties for the boys—
and good luck!"

We sang "We Wish You a Merry Christmas"
with all the verses—Miss Hauser was a great be-
liever in singing all the verses—and then we folded
up our music and began to make our way down the
risers.

I watched as Zandra and her gang walked down
the wooden planks. The Purple Sweater was step-
ping down sideways so that her back was to me. I
could tell she was mad and that she was planning
something just by the way her large shoulders were
hunched up and by the way she was gesturing to
the four girls beside her.

I knew that if I was ever going to say something
to Zandra, I was going to have to say it now. But
Miss Hauser was still there at the piano, answering
questions. I couldn't say anything with Miss Hauser
still there. And Zandra and her gang had stepped

off the risers and were putting their music on top of the piano.

Then Miss Hauser disappeared. Someone must have needed something from the office and she and the two girls who had been standing by her were no longer in the auditorium.

Half the chorus had already left, but there was still a good number of kids hanging around. This was just what I had been waiting for—no teacher, lots of kids. I took a breath.

"Hey, Zandra."

The Purple Sweater turned around. She looked surprised. Then she smiled a little sly smile. Two of her gang stood on either side of her. Nobody else paid any attention. Kids were piling their music up, plinking on the piano, talking.

"Hey, Zandra," I said a little louder. "Are you going to bully me today?"

"What?" Zandra said this as if it were the furthest thing from her mind.

"I said, are you going to bully me today?" I repeated loudly.

The plinking on the piano stopped. Some kids froze in the middle of putting on their sweaters.

"You know exactly what I'm talking about, Zandra Kott. You'd love to get me out on that yard and beat up on me, wouldn't you? You'd love to make fun of me, wouldn't you?"

The auditorium was quiet. Zandra's eyes were as

big as planets. She took a step forward and then began to rock from side to side on her heels. She realized she couldn't do anything with all these kids looking at us. By this time, we were in the middle of a large semicircle.

"And it's easy to make fun of me, isn't it," I said. Unlike Zandra, I wasn't rocking at all. There was no melted cheese. I felt as if my toes had spread roots out under the auditorium's floor. I could have stood there forever.

"It's easy to make fun of me and bully me because you've got your gang." I didn't mind getting snide. "You've got four girls around you who act like you're some kind of . . . of . . ." Then it came to me: "Animal trainer."

The four girls let their mouths fall open. The Boxer looked at Zandra. Zandra just stared straight ahead.

"And why do you make fun of *me*? Why do you beat up on *me*?"

"I—" Zandra began.

"Why am I the *only* person in this *whole school* you can bully? Huh, Zandra? Shall I tell everyone in this room *why*?"

Suddenly, Zandra began to cry. She didn't make a sound, but her huge green eyes were brimming with tears that rolled down her cheeks like fat rain-drops. Please, please, please, her eyes begged me, don't say I'm Jewish. *Please*.

109

"Because," I said, "because—"

And then I saw something I had never seen before—the Purple Sweater was just this chunky girl in a ratty old cardigan who was scared and sad about herself. And stuck with a mom who was probably crazy and missing a dad she wasn't going to see for a long, long time.

Zandra had now closed her eyes and her face was wet and shiny. I noticed a tiny brown freckle on one of Zandra's damp eyelids. Like Shirley Klein's . . . What had Shirley said? *Beser der* . . . Better that . . . "Better that my enemy should see good in me than I see evil in him." Zandra didn't look so evil anymore. Just frightened and alone.

The whole auditorium was waiting for me to go on.

"Because we're the same," I said finally. "Because inside we're exactly the same. Did you listen to my song?" Zandra nodded and rocked back and forth on her heels.

And that was it. I didn't say anything else. Some of the kids who had watched all of this came up to me and said something, but most everyone else slowly walked away. The four girls next to Zandra finished putting on their jackets and left. The janitor came in with his trash bin and broom.

Zandra looked as if she had been holding her breath this whole time. Then she walked back across the auditorium to the far side of the stage where

there were three little steps that led to a door marked
EMERGENCY EXIT. This door opened directly onto the
street behind the school. There would be no playground to cross.

"Hey!" the janitor shouted as Zandra opened the
door. "You're not supposed to—" But the girl who
wore a purple sweater was gone.

Chapter Twelve

MRS. Vanderbuildt pointed an index finger to her forehead. "Oh, you know what, children? I just remembered that we forgot to finish our angels!" Our class must have given Mrs. Vanderbuildt a look that said *what angels?* because she added, "Our aluminum foil angels, the ones we cut out on the day we had that awful Take Cover Drill. They need cotton ball clouds to stand on and fly around in!"

The Take Cover Drill had been two weeks ago and even though Christmas vacation was on Friday and this was already late Tuesday, everyone got out their scissors. In Mrs. Vanderbuildt's class, you got used to doing things according to Mrs. Vanderbuildt's memory.

"Edith! Nick! Fetch the art supplies, please!"

I joined Nick at the back of the room.

"Hey, Edith," Nick said as he opened up the art cupboard.

"Hey, yourself," I said to Nick. The more I looked at Nick, the more I decided he didn't look like Clint Eastwood on *Rawhide* after all, but that he was handsome, anyway.

"I've been carrying around that stupid old pod from the Hopscotch Tree ever since our game with Mrs. Sutton's class and I ain't got no luck. Here." He handed me a tray of plastic bottles filled with white glue.

"Nick! Edith! Hurry up back there! We've only got a few minutes until school's out!" Mrs. Vanderbuildt said nervously. We passed out all the bottles and returned to the cupboard.

"Well, what happened to you?" I whispered to Nick. "Anything bad?"

Nick reached into the art shelves. "For one thing, my brother and me get into these fights and my mom yells at us a lot."

"Didn't that go on before? I mean, before you got the pod?" I asked.

"Yeah, but nothing good has happened."

"Like what, for instance?"

Nick piled the cotton wads and pieces of cardboard onto my arms. "Like a tractor. I wanted a tractor."

"Nick," I said. "I told you—it doesn't work like that."

Nick winked one of his great winks at me. "Well, you got a rabbit!"

"Children!" Mrs. Vanderbuildt called out. "The rest of us are waiting!"

When I got back to my seat, Rita had already traded places with one of The Cathys so she could sit next to me.

"I asked the Hopscotch Tree something about a certain someone this morning," she said. Rita was doing this a lot lately—just saying enough to tease me about what she asked the Hopscotch Tree and then not telling me the rest. I looked over at Nick. He was concentrating so hard on his cotton cloud that his great, dark eyebrows had come together in one straight line across his forehead.

"Maybe I should ask the Hopscotch Tree about a certain someone," I said. Rita looked across the room and then back at me and giggled. "Ooh, Edith, you don't have to," she said. "I think he likes you."

I put down my cardboard. "You do? He does?" I felt my ears and cheeks turn warm. I tried to hurry up and finish my angel so that I could give it to Nick.

"Yes, I do-ooo," Rita sang. She pulled on one of her earrings. "You know, Edith, I changed my mind. I think Chanukah whatchamacallits—"

"*Gelt,*" I said.

"*Gelt,*" repeated Rita, "win the dessert contest."

My mouth dropped open. I stared at Rita as if she had just told me I had finally, for the first time ever, *won* the dessert contest—which she had just told me!

"Well," Rita explained, "Chanukah *gelt* are so pretty, number one. I mean, they look just like little gold coins, in that cute little net bag. And, number two, they're chocolate and they're sooo good! Besides, my doughnuts were stale anyway."

I laughed—and then I thought of something.

"Hey, Rita—"

"Hay is for horses," Rita said.

"Would you go to a Chanukah party with me at the Vermont Avenue Jewish Center? And what are you doing with the glue?"

"I'm pouring it on my finger so I can peel it off later when it dries. Sure, I'll go. When—"

And then, of course, the bell rang.

"Oh, dear," Mrs. Vanderbuildt said, sighing. "This always happens, doesn't it? Will someone remind me tomorrow? Or after the Christmas concert tonight?"

"I will," Leonard Mooner volunteered. But no one else paid any attention. We all left the cotton wads, glue, and cardboard on our desks and ran out the door.

"I'll tell you about the party tomorrow, Rita!" I yelled as she ran down the hall to meet her sisters. I looked around for Nick, but he had disappeared.

I looked across the playground at the Hopscotch Tree. The leaves were flapping and fluttering to me. *Come closer*, it said, *come closer*. I walked toward the Tree and stopped. There was someone there ahead of me, whispering into the knot with the hole in it, and looking up through the branches to see the reply. It was Zandra. I waited until I saw the Tree answer her. It was still for a moment, and then said, *No*. I walked over.

"Hi," I said.

Zandra looked down at the hopscotch squares and scuffed a shoe along the cracked yellow lines. "Hi," she said. I could barely hear her.

I didn't know what to say. Maybe if she knew about talking to the Tree, she should know about the rest.

"Did you pick up a seed pod?" I asked. "Sometimes that helps you out."

She dug into her sweater and showed me a thick end of a pod. "Yeah," she said.

I sat down on the bench. I hadn't expected to see Zandra here and I didn't know what she had expected. Both of us were real uncomfortable with the other, but neither of us was going to leave. So she stood and looked at the ground while I sat and watched her for what seemed a long, long time. Then she looked up at me.

"Tonight's the first night of Chanukah," she said.

"Yeah," I said. "We'll probably light the meno-rah first and then have dinner and then come back to school for the concert. My mom makes *great* latkes—"

Zandra bit her lip and looked down again. I stopped. Now why was I talking about my mom and Chanukah and stuff in front of Zandra? "Do you ... do you do anything for Chanukah?" I asked. I watched the top of Zandra's head answer me.

"I ... yeah, we did ... we used to celebrate Christmas, too, with my dad." Zandra's green eyes stared right past me. "I want to be with my dad. Even if he moved out on us, I want to be with him." Zandra focused back on me.

"And I want to be Catholic, like my dad."

All of a sudden, I remembered what it felt like to be the only Jew cutting out angels in Mrs. Vander-buildt's class. But still ...

The Tree rustled and swayed.

"... why should you hide/The magic inside/That's there for me and for you ..." I softly sang.

Zandra turned away.

I didn't know what else to do, and I guess Zandra didn't either. I looked down on the bench where I was sitting and waited.

I thought again about the concert.

"Do you have a white blouse?"

"Uh-huh," Zandra said, and faced me once more, "but it's too tight."

I smiled. "Mine's too tight, too."

Zandra grinned.

"Doosh-sheesh-ka!"

I turned around. There was Daddy's faded green paint truck parked at the back gate. I remembered he wasn't working. That's why I was getting picked up so early.

"Well—" I said. I stood up and brushed the bench dirt off the back of my pleated skirt.

"Edith," Zandra said. "I . . . Happy Chanukah."

"Happy Chanukah to you, Zandra," I said.

She ran a finger up and down the trunk of the Hopscotch Tree.

"Thanks," she said and looked away.

I walked out of the playground and climbed into my father's truck. Daddy scrunched the gears together and cocked his head in the direction of the schoolyard.

"Who's that?" he asked. "A friend?"

"No," I said as we pulled away. "Just a girl I know."

I twisted around on the seat so that I could see out the small rounded windows at the back of the truck. Zandra had spread her arms across the Hopscotch Tree and the Tree was beckoning me back. Branches upon branches and leaves upon leaves were reaching out and then bending in long, curling waves. *Come back*, it was calling, *come back*.

I will, I said silently, *I will*.

ABOUT THE AUTHOR

A former professional actress and teacher, Ms. Siskind is currently an intern therapist in child psychotherapy. She resides in Los Angeles with her husband and daughter. *The Hopscotch Tree* has lived in her heart a long time and is her first book.